Tainted Obsession

King of Ruin
Book One

Julia Sykes

Copyright © 2024 by Julia Sykes

All rights reserved.

No part of this book may be reproduced in any form or by any electronic or mechanical means, including information storage and retrieval systems, without written permission from the author, except for the use of brief quotations in a book review.

Cover Design by Mayhem Cover Creations

Chapter 1

Evelyn

The thick cloth gag between my teeth trapped my tongue, smothering my pleas for mercy. My breath stuttered, and my chest heaved on short, shallow gasps. I jerked against the restraints that bound my wrists and ankles. Zip ties dug into my flesh, the unyielding bonds tearing my skin as I struggled for freedom. At some point, my relentless screams had broken down into ragged shouts, my ravaged throat becoming raw and hoarse.

I had no idea how much time had passed since I'd been taken. All I remembered were the strong arms that'd grabbed me from behind and the acrid smell of the cloth that'd been shoved over my nose and mouth. I'd been leaving work, following the familiar path from the university back to my apartment. Then everything had dissolved into darkness.

It was still dark; no light slipped through the blindfold that was knotted tightly enough to make my head ache. The damp concrete floor was cool beneath my cheek, but the chilly sensation did nothing to soothe the pounding in my brain.

I couldn't see, couldn't move, couldn't speak. The sense of complete helplessness crushed my chest like a lead weight, preventing my lungs from fully expanding. Razor sharp fear clawed at my mind, shredding my thoughts.

"Shut up!" The man's frustrated bark hit me at the same time his boot slammed into my stomach.

My insides writhed in agony, and my shouts were silenced as I choked for air.

"Don't kill her," another man warned. "We need her as a hostage."

The first man had yelled at me in English, but the second man spoke Spanish. They had to be aware I was American, even though I'd done my best to acclimate to life in Mexico City and was fluent in Spanish. The prospect that they knew I was an expat chilled my blood. And they'd mentioned keeping me as a hostage. How much did these men know about me?

I feared I already knew why they'd abducted me,

but my brain refused to fully acknowledge the horror of my situation; I was too absorbed in processing the pain of the brutal kick to the gut.

They continued to discuss me in their native language. "Crawford will come for her. Then we can kill them both."

A strangled sound caught in my throat. I couldn't have begged for George's life even if I wanted to. *Crawford.* They were talking about my fiancé. George was a DEA agent. We'd moved to Mexico City for his job. If these men wanted to get to him, then they must be affiliated with one of the cartels he fought against on a daily basis.

"No reason I can't have a little fun before he gets here." Rough hands grabbed me, groping at my chest.

Horror twisted my stomach. I tried to shriek, but I managed little more than a pained wheeze. My insides were still on fire, and my diaphragm wouldn't expand to draw in a full breath.

I thrashed, the cable ties ripping at the skin around my wrists and ankles. The man's breath was hot and putrid on my cheek. Acting on instinct, I slammed my head in his direction. Pain lanced my skull at the impact, and a flash of bright light flickered over my dark world as my head spun.

The man's sickening heat receded, and his string of

curses boomed through the cramped space where they were holding me captive.

"What the fuck are you doing?" A new, deep voice cracked across my flickering consciousness. "Who is she?"

There was something odd about his accented Spanish, but my mind was spinning too fast to contemplate it.

"She's George Crawford's fiancée." Someone spat on the concrete. "He'll come for her, and we'll kill that motherfucker."

Cold flashed over me at the threat to George's life, and my struggles became more frantic. I didn't notice the blood that welled around my restraints, coating my palms in warmth. I tried to beg for his life, to rail at these monsters that I wouldn't let them use me against my fiancé.

"She broke my fucking nose." I recognized the voice of the man who'd groped me, but it was slightly more nasal now. "She'll pay for that."

Pain exploded through my head, and a wave of nausea crashed over me. A furious roar resounded through the cramped space, the primal sound all that tethered me to reality as my consciousness wavered.

Chapter 2

Massimo

Acting without thinking, I grabbed the motherfucker who'd kicked a defenseless woman and slammed him back against the wall. His head made a satisfying *crack* against the concrete blocks, and his dark eyes slid out of focus. My knife was at his throat in a heartbeat, drawn from the sheath at my side in one lighting fast, practiced sweep.

"Let him go!" his friend shouted at me in Spanish. It wasn't my native language, but I'd made sure to learn it before traveling here from Italy.

I stayed my hand just before my blade opened his throat, summoning all my willpower to prevent myself from killing the coward. What kind of man kicked a bound and helpless woman, especially one as fragile as the willowy blonde who was now far too still on the damp floor?

Not a man at all. I appraised the two pieces of shit in the cramped basement with me. Both watched me with wide, terrified eyes. They were little more than boys, barely in their twenties. I could handle them easily if necessary.

"What the fuck do you think you're doing?" I seethed, pressing my blade just deep enough to draw a drop of ruby blood from my enemy's throat.

No. Not my enemy, I reminded myself. These men worked for Stefano Duarte, my new ally. They'd called me here for a meeting, promising a gift.

Whatever the fuck this was, I didn't want it. I didn't give a damn if the woman had murdered one of their mothers; I didn't brutalize women. They could've ended her quickly if it was necessary to eliminate her, but they'd chosen to have a little fun with her first.

"Why did you call me to come here?" I narrowed my eyes at the man who was barely breathing beneath my blade. "And why the fuck would you think I would thank you for hurting her?"

"I told you," the other man said quickly, his voice shaking slightly. "She's George Crawford's fiancée. The boss wants him eliminated. And we know that you're in Mexico City to do business with him. We want in on your new operation." He licked his lips and hurried on. "We'll help you get on good terms with Duarte, and you can count on us to establish your business in Mexico."

The one in my murderous grip swallowed hard but lifted his chin in a show of bravado. "Crawford will come for her, and you can help us kill him. Then, we'll all earn Duarte's favor. We'll all be rich. That's why you came here from Naples, isn't it?"

The woman stirred on a low moan, a wordless protest to the threat against her fiancé.

I bared my teeth at him as rage rose in my chest, threatening to take hold and drive me to reckless violence.

"She's innocent?" I growled the question, and my blade pressed deeper into his flesh.

"She's in love with that motherfucker," the other man protested. "Why should we give a shit about her?"

"I asked you a question," I hissed. "Is she innocent?"

"Aren't you listening? We'll all be richer than gods. She's nothing, no one. I'm not going to let some bitch stop me from getting paid."

He kicked her again, taking out his frustration with me on her fragile form. She went as still as a broken doll, and blood welled from a cut on her forehead.

A red haze descended over my mind, obliterating rational thought entirely. If I took a moment to think, I would remember my mission here in Mexico City. I'd think twice about crossing Stefano Duarte, the powerful drug lord who commanded these abusive bastards.

But I'd never been a cautious man, and my instinct for vicious, efficient violence had kept me alive in situations far more dangerous than this one.

I was the danger in this dank basement; the two young men who shared the cramped space were little more than boys.

But they were old enough to kidnap and brutalize an innocent woman.

They would die for that.

I didn't give a fuck that George Crawford was a dirty agent, and Duarte wanted his head for helping a rival cartel. I didn't care that I needed an alliance with Duarte to further my own ambitions. All that mattered was punishing these motherfuckers, eliminating them so they could never hurt an innocent woman again.

My world was steeped in blood and sin, but I never victimized civilians. I didn't allow it back home in

Naples, and I wouldn't stand by and watch it happen here in Mexico, no matter how badly I needed Duarte's friendship.

With one clean swipe of my blade, I opened the pinned man's throat. I dropped him like the trash he was, not bothering to watch the light leave his eyes. The gory choking sound of his final moments faded to a familiar, macabre beat in the background of my murderous fury. Despite the volatile emotion that'd taken hold of my psyche, my movements were controlled and precise as I turned to face my surviving enemy. His mouth opened to beg for his miserable life, but my knife had already left my fingers. It embedded itself deep in his chest, hitting the target of his heart with perfect precision.

He dropped to his knees, gaping at me in shock. His pathetic attempts to draw his final breaths would've been almost comical if it weren't for the severity of his crime. The bastard deserved to die screaming, but I'd ended the fight before it could truly begin. I had enough rationality remaining to know that I couldn't risk drawing the attention of the authorities if anyone heard their dying cries. That instinct for survival had kept me alive this long, and I didn't intend to end up in prison in Mexico. I would never risk being caged again.

I shook the remaining violent tension from my shoulders and plucked my blade from the dying man's chest. The threat had been handled. The woman was all that mattered now.

She was too still, and the pool of crimson blood beneath her pale cheek stained her white-blonde hair. She was small and slender, appearing as frail as a broken butterfly. More blood coated her hands where she'd torn her wrists fighting the cruel restraints that the bastards had used to incapacitate her.

I crouched over her and tested her pulse at her throat. It was steady beneath my fingers. I heaved out a breath, the last of my rage leaving my body on a long exhale. The men who'd hurt her were dead. No one would harm her now.

Moving with the swiftness of familiarity, I freed the knotted gag and blindfold. She didn't stir when they dropped away from her face. Long lashes fanned her lightly freckled cheeks, and her eyes remained closed. She was beautiful and delicate and far too pale.

I hissed a curse and wiped the dead man's blood from my knife before using it to cut away the cable ties around her ankles and wrists. She didn't so much as flinch when I carefully peeled them from her torn skin.

I had to get her to a hospital. Dropping her off myself would be a stupid risk, so I put in an anonymous call to emergency services and gave them our location.

I waited with her until I heard the wail of approaching sirens. Then I took a breath and forced myself to leave her alone in the basement with the lifeless bodies of my enemies. I couldn't allow the authorities to find me here. The ambulance would be here soon, and she would get the medical care she needed.

Besides, if I wanted to check on her wellbeing in the coming days, I knew exactly where to find her. She was George Crawford's fiancée. I would make amends to Duarte by offering to stalk his DEA agent enemy myself. And if I was able to watch over this innocent beauty at the same time, all the better. Her piece of shit lover wouldn't be alive much longer. Until then, I could protect her from my criminal associates.

Chapter 3

Evelyn

Fear seized my mind in a vise grip before I stirred to full consciousness. Disjointed, horrific memories flickered through my thoughts in a nauseating film reel.

Darkness. Terror. Pain. Hands groping at my body, violating me while I was bound and helpless. Unable to move or scream for help.

George. They wanted to kill my fiancé. They were using me as bait to lure him into a trap.

I jolted upright with a gasp, and pain knifed through my skull. The overly bright world swirled around me, and I fell back onto the pillow.

I was laying on something soft, not damp concrete. My head pounded, but no further agony was inflicted as punishment for my struggles. My hands twitched at my sides, jerking against the phantom restraints that no longer bound me.

"George." I moaned his name, fear for him saturating my thoughts.

"I'm right here." His warm, familiar hand settled gently over mine, the barest brush of his palm against my knuckles.

"George." This time, his name was a harsh sob. I turned my hand so that I could clutch at him, holding on like he was my lifeline.

"You're safe now," he promised, his voice tight with suppressed anger.

I blinked hard, forcing my heavy lids to open so that I could find his steady blue gaze. His soft navy eyes filled my world, and I quickly dashed away the sting of tears before my vision blurred. I couldn't lose sight of him.

My wrist ached as I moved to wipe the wetness from my cheeks, and I noted the thick white bandage that encircled it. I glanced down at our entwined hands and saw that both wrists had been similarly dressed; the wounds inflicted by the cruel cable ties had been treated.

The bright, clinical lighting and slightly harsh, sterile scent in the air told me that I was in a hospital. Not a dank basement.

"You saved me," I rasped, my throat still hoarse from screaming.

Fine lines of strain tightened around George's mouth, his expression turning stony. The familiar, smooth planes of his classically handsome face hardened into rough-hewn granite. Six years ago, I'd fallen hard for his captain-of-the-football team sunny smile and golden hair. But I'd learned to read his darker moods in the subtle shifts of his square jaw and the shadowed dimple in his chin. George was tense, on the edge of fury.

"You're safe now," he repeated.

"How did you find me? Those men. They wanted to kill you." I jolted upright again, wincing at the sudden stab of pain through my skull. I breathed through it and frantically appraised him, searching for signs of injury. "Are you hurt?"

"No, baby. I'm fine." He reassured me, but he remained tense. I sensed an intangible distance between us, the one that separated our hearts when he was in one of his particularly prickly moods.

"But how...?" I clutched at his hand more tightly, desperate to pull him closer and bridge the invisible barrier between us. "What happened? The last thing I remember..."

I trailed off on a shudder, not wanting to think

about the awful ordeal. The phantom taint of the man's hands pawing at my breasts made my stomach twist, and nausea rolled through me.

George's long fingers finally gripped mine with equal force. "I need *you* to tell me what happened," he said, voice still tight with barely leashed, volatile emotion. "You were late coming home to make dinner, and the next thing I knew, I was getting a phone call saying you're in the hospital." He raked a hand through his sandy blond hair. "They told me they found you in a basement with two dead men. Someone put in an anonymous emergency call to get an ambulance to your location. What the hell happened?"

My heart pounded with remembered terror, but I forced my mind to focus on the fear-drenched memories in order to puzzle out my situation. George needed the information so that he could go after the men who'd taken me. He just wanted to protect me.

I reached out and traced the line of his clean-shaven jaw, trying to soothe away his tension. "I'm okay," I promised. "I'm with you now."

He blew out a long breath and turned his face into my touch, so he could brush a kiss over my palm. "I didn't know where you were," he admitted, his voice shaking slightly. "You scared me, baby."

"I'm okay," I repeated, drawn to comfort him. I

hated the thorny mood that'd created a painful gulf between us. I needed him now more than ever. "Hold me?" I asked, my voice small and embarrassingly weak.

He sighed again and wrapped his arms around me, drawing me into a careful embrace. I shuddered as the residual horror of my ordeal washed through me, and my tears wet his shirt. I buried my face in his chest and clutched at him, weaving my fingers through his thick, wavy hair to hold him close.

His heartbeat was strong and steady beneath my ear, the beat reassuring me.

Alive. George was alive, and so was I.

"What happened, Evie?" he asked, more gently this time.

"I..." I swallowed the acid tang on my tongue and forced myself to remember. "I was on my way home from the university after I finished my classes for the day."

George's hand tightened around mine. "I told you not to walk on your own," he reprimanded.

"I was only going to the bus stop," I said, a bit defensive. I hadn't defied George's warnings and wandered through the unfamiliar streets by myself. I knew the route to work using the bus, but I wasn't confident navigating Mexico City on foot; George was too busy with work to show me around, and it would be stupid of me to risk getting lost on my own. The cartels might know my fiancé's job with the DEA and target me.

A shudder wracked my body. That was exactly what had happened.

"Who took you?" he demanded. "Which cartel was responsible?"

"I..." I searched my dark memories for any clues about the identities of the men who'd taken me. "I don't know."

His lips thinned. "You're fluent in Spanish, Evie. You teach English at the university for god's sake. You must have been able to understand what they were saying around you."

"They drugged me somehow. And when I woke up, I was blindfolded and gagged. They didn't talk to me," I blurted in an awful rush of remembered terror. "All they talked about was how they were going to use me as bait to get to you. They wanted to kill you, George."

I wrapped my arms around his shoulders, clinging to him so that I could continue to feel his heartbeat against me. It quickened with anxiety for my distress, but his hold on me remained firm and reassuring.

"But who were they?" he insisted. "I have to know,

baby. It's the only way I can protect us. I can arrest the men responsible, and we'll be safe."

I shook my head against his chest. "I don't know. I'm sorry. I don't know."

His strong arms flexed around me. "How did those men end up dead in that basement with you? Who called for the ambulance?"

Guilt twisted my gut. "I don't know," I said again, useless. "I couldn't see any of them. They said…"

"What did they say?" he prompted when I hesitated.

I forced myself to sort through the jumbled memories of agony and fear. "There were two men with me in the basement, and then a third man spoke. He asked if I was innocent. He seemed angry."

A shudder raced through me as the feral roar of rage echoed through my mind. Despite my residual terror, I knew deep in my bones that the third man had saved me. He'd killed his associates and set me free.

"Then one of them…hurt me," I forced myself to say, skipping over the part where they'd tried to violate me. George didn't need to know about that. It would only upset him more.

I gingerly touched the aching spot on my forehead. "I blacked out. I don't know what happened after that. The next thing I knew, I was here with you." I hugged him impossibly tighter. "You're alive." My voice hitched, and fresh tears wet his shirt.

They hadn't killed my fiancé. He was warm and vital in my arms, heart beating steadily once again.

"You scared me, baby," he confessed, a rare moment of vulnerability.

Guilt clawed at me. "I'm okay," I promised again. "I'll be more careful."

"I should keep you at the apartment," he rumbled. "I never should have agreed to allow you to teach at the university."

"We need the money," I countered. We were saving to buy our own home back in Albuquerque one day. We were partners, and I had to contribute to our future.

He grimaced. "I don't want you going anywhere alone anymore. It's not safe for you here."

For a brief, selfish moment, I hoped he was going to declare that we were returning to New Mexico.

But I couldn't allow him to abandon his aspirations with the DEA. George had always wanted to be in law enforcement, to be a force for good in this world. I had to support that noble dream.

"I'll be more careful," I vowed.

He pulled away from me, a small frown twisting his lips with disapproval. "Be honest with me, Evie.

You weren't going straight to the bus stop, were you? You were taking pictures again."

The awful truth pierced my heart. I had paused to take some photos as I strolled to the bus stop. I'd promised George that I wouldn't go out into the city with my camera like I would when I'd lived in Albuquerque, but sometimes I saw the perfect shot, and I pulled out my phone to capture the moment.

"I just stopped for a few minutes," I protested. "I didn't wander through the streets or anything."

But even as I spoke, my cheeks heated with shame. This was all my fault.

My distraction had cost me dearly. I'd let my guard down to indulge my art, and I'd made myself an easy target.

My dreams of being a professional photographer had always been foolish, and now, playing pretend had almost cost George's life.

"I won't do it ever again," I swore. "I'm sorry."

He blew out a long sigh, and the frown mostly eased from his handsome features, his expression mercifully softening. "I know you won't. I think you know better now and will take my warnings seriously. Won't you?"

I nodded quickly. "Yes," I agreed. "I won't mess up again. I won't put you in danger, George."

He brushed an approving kiss over my aching forehead, and warmth settled over me despite the brief flicker of pain. George was with me, and we were both alive. Safe.

I would do anything to protect him, even if that meant giving up my small pleasures. I could go back to my photography hobby once we moved back to the States. It wasn't as though I would ever make a career with my art. It was just a silly way I liked to express my irrepressible creative streak. It'd always been an impractical indulgence, and now, it'd almost gotten both of us killed.

I would be more vigilant from now on.

"You should quit your job," he said, and cold panic pulsed through me. "Your small paycheck isn't worth risking our lives."

"No!" I took a breath to calm my nerves. "Please, George. I can't just stay in that apartment all the time."

I wasn't particularly extroverted—George was the only real friend I'd ever had—but the apartment was small and cramped. The dangers of the city hemmed me in even more. I couldn't bear to be trapped inside, locked away from the beauty and the ugliness of the world. All facets of humanity fascinated me. Even if I was apart from the emotional bonds most people easily enjoyed, I was able to observe it all through the lens of my camera.

"You wouldn't be in the apartment all the time. We'll still go to the market together," George allowed.

The only time I got to take my camera out was on our weekly trips to the market, when George made time away from work to accompany me. Otherwise, my commute to the university allowed me a small window into the world. If I lost that, I would go crazy from the isolation.

"That's once a week," I said weakly, feeling selfish that I was protesting when he only wanted to protect us both.

He raked a hand through his sandy hair, mussing it from its usual tidy style. He only did that when he was deeply frustrated with me, and the gesture made me cringe internally.

"I'll spend more time with you," he promised. "You can come with me when I'm networking socially. But you're not going to the university anymore. Not by yourself. And I can't leave work to escort you around the city every day."

Anguish crushed my heart, but I couldn't defy him. He was only being reasonable, responsible for our safety.

We wouldn't be in Mexico City forever. I could deal with the temporary isolation.

"You'd be okay with me going to the bar with you and your friends?" I asked cautiously.

George usually didn't want me around when he was establishing his career connections. Going out for drinks and forming friendships was an important part of advancement in his line of work. The camaraderie he shared with his fellow agents also kept us in a tight-knit community that added another layer of protection. We were outsiders here, and the nature of George's work made us enemies of the cartels.

He nodded tightly. "I can keep an eye on you when we go out," he said. "Besides, a couple of the other wives come out with us sometimes."

"They do?" I asked breathlessly, hope budding in my chest.

I didn't make friends easily, but female company would be nice. Especially if I was going to be confined to the apartment for most of every day.

He nodded again, that awful frown still tugging at the corners of his mouth.

"Thank you," I said fervently. "I'll be safe as long as I'm with you."

I knew that truth deep in my bones. George was my *person*. He was my everything, my entire world. He wouldn't allow anyone to take me from him ever again. Besides, he couldn't keep me safe if I made foolish, headstrong choices. I wouldn't fight him on this anymore. I would quit my job and make the shabby little apartment into a home for us.

"Do as I say, and you'll be safe," he said. "I can't protect you if you get reckless and go off on your own to take your pictures."

"I won't," I agreed.

He hugged me again, and I leaned into his chest. He shushed me gently and rubbed his hand up and down my back in a soothing motion.

"We won't be here forever, baby," he reassured me. "Just a year or two until I get promoted."

I nodded, hardening my resolve. I could stay mostly isolated for that period of time. To keep George safe, I would sacrifice anything.

Chapter 4

Massimo

"I thought we were going to be friends, Massimo. I welcomed you into my home, but now you've killed two of my men." Stefano Duarte cocked his head at me, his genial expression belied by the dangerous flash of white-hot anger over his black eyes, keen and dangerous as a shark. The defined lines of his cheekbones and jaw were drawn tight, sharp enough to cut. "I thought we were going to have a very profitable relationship."

The back of my neck prickled with awareness of a threat, an ingrained response to mortal danger. Duarte only had two silent, burly guards stationed in his lavish study where he'd arranged this meeting, but we were in the heart of his criminal empire. The opulence of the space only enhanced his aura of power—from the crimson leather armchair he sat upon like a throne to the cut crystal glass of fine whiskey that dangled nonchalantly in his hand.

In contrast, my friends and I stood, awaiting his judgment.

His next words could sign our death warrants. Dozens of lethally armed killers were stationed throughout the high rise building that the drug lord owned. If we tried to fight our way out, we wouldn't survive the attempt.

Enzo and Gian tensed at my back, the brothers bracing for a fight. They would defend me with their lives, even though I'd been the one to recklessly put us in this dangerous position.

Everything we'd ever wanted was within our grasp—money, power, security—and I might've fucked it all up. We would be lucky to get out of here alive after my slight to Duarte, the most notorious, mercurial drug lord in Mexico.

He leaned forward in his armchair, bracing his elbows on his knees as he skewered me with a lethal stare. A lock of night-black hair fell over his brow, and he casually smoothed it into its effortlessly swept-back style. That sleek panther's grace set my teeth on edge, an effect he carefully cultivated to intimidate his enemies.

Gian would be better equipped to talk his way out of this than I was. He could wield his tongue as effectively as I handled my knives. That was how we'd survived this long.

But this was my mess. I wouldn't allow my friends to die because of my actions. My decision to save the woman—Evelyn Day, George Crawford's fiancée—had been impulsive, instinctual. I'd learned that she was innocent, and my own demons had overwhelmed my better judgment.

"Enzo and Gian had nothing to do with this," I asserted, lifting my chin to meet Duarte's sharp glare with defiance. "I killed your men. It was my call."

Dark brows arched over the drug lord's keen eyes, a promise of death lurking in the black pools. "Is there a reason you chose to insult me like this?" he drawled, outwardly cool and composed.

"Your *men*," I spat the word with disdain, "were brutalizing an innocent woman. They kidnapped George Crawford's fiancée. They beat her and were going to do far worse if I hadn't stopped them." I squared my shoulders. "That's not how I do business in Naples."

Duarte's lips thinned. "You're not in Naples," he said coldly. "This is my territory. You are my guest."

"She's innocent." I held my ground. "Crawford

might be a piece of shit, but she didn't deserve that. Your men were going to kill her after she served her purpose as bait."

"And you care so much about an innocent woman being hurt?" he challenged coolly, expression unreadable.

"Yes," I bit out, bracing for violence. I'd admitted to my crime against him, and I wouldn't apologize for it.

A grim smile sharpened Duarte's features, his sudden shift in demeanor knocking me off balance. "Good. That's not how I do business, either. Besides, Carmen would've had my balls if I'd allowed an innocent woman to suffer like that under my watch. You've saved my marriage, Massimo." He tipped his head at me. "You have my gratitude. If those bastards were still alive, they'd be thanking you for ending them far more quickly than I would have."

I released a long breath, struggling to ease the tension from my muscles. Seconds ago, I'd been prepared to fight for my life. Now, Duarte was beaming at me like I was his closest friend in the world. The cartel boss had earned his mercurial reputation. It was unnerving as hell.

I could respect that. A partnership with such a man would enrich us all.

And he'd just proven that he had his own code of honor that was closely aligned with mine. We would have a profitable alliance. I wouldn't return home to Naples until we'd sealed our bargain.

"If he's your enemy, I'll personally take care of George Crawford," I vowed.

I wouldn't apologize for killing Duarte's men, but I could make amends.

"A very generous offer," he drawled. "Are you not worried about drawing the attention of the DEA to your organization?"

Enzo and Gian both took a step forward at the same time in a show of solidarity. But despite their physical demonstration of loyalty, my friends weren't keen to anger the American feds. Not when we hadn't even sealed our deal with Duarte to establish a cocaine trafficking route back to Italy. Our position here was tenuous, the alliance new and fragile. We didn't yet have the infrastructure in Mexico and Colombia to defend our interests.

It was up to me, in this moment, to ensure Duarte's friendship. He was the key to securing the alliance with his Colombian partners. We needed them all if we were going to pull off our coup.

Gian's anvil jaw ticked, a rare sign of frustration. He usually concealed his more volatile emotions, his stoic bearing matching his military-rigid style. For him, it was tantamount to an enraged outburst. Otherwise, he remained outwardly composed, his dark green eyes steady on Duarte.

Enzo wasn't quite as skilled at hiding his feelings. His body swelled, his bulk obvious even in his sharply tailored suit. The scar that curved beneath his right cheekbone was drawn deep on a frown, his displeasure so clear that the mark was visible past the fall of wavy black hair that he grew long to cover it.

The brothers might give me hell for making this risky call later, in private, but my instincts had kept me alive for this long. I would trust in them now.

"We're friends, aren't we?" I asked Duarte. "Friends watch each other's backs. If George Crawford is causing problems for you, I'll eliminate him."

His eyes glinted with satisfaction. "All right, Massimo. I accept your gesture of friendship." He swirled the whiskey in his cut crystal glass, drawing out a moment of silence before divulging more. With every heartbeat, the tension in the room grew thicker. The man knew how to create an intimidating atmosphere, I'd give him that.

I met his dark stare head-on.

"We're glad to hear that," Gian offered, stepping in to navigate the politics of the situation. With his general's bearing, he commanded, "Tell us what we can do to help."

"You and I have a lot of business to discuss, Gian," Duarte countered, still smiling. "I'm sure Massimo can deal with this little problem on his own."

It was a decree, not a suggestion. It seemed I was to be rebuked for the insult of murdering his men, even if he would've made the same judgment call. I understood the slight to his honor; I should've presented the bastards to him so that he could handle them personally.

I would pay my dues and make amends to Duarte by taking on the risk alone.

"Yes," I agreed firmly before Enzo and Gian could declare that they would help me take on the DEA. "My friends have a lot to discuss with you. They're the brains behind this operation. I can deal with Crawford on my own."

Duarte chuckled, eyes roving over all six foot five of my bulky frame. "I'm sure you can."

It was true; we were in Mexico because of my friends' aspirations, not mine. I didn't care as much about making this power move in order to overthrow our boss back home. All I cared about was my freedom and security. And defending my friends, who were as close as brothers. I'd taken my part in this risky plot because it would further their ends. The coup mattered to them, and keeping them alive mattered to me. I would die for Enzo and Gian, but if all went to plan, we wouldn't just survive; we would prosper. We'd all be richer and more powerful than I'd ever dared to dream.

Duarte leaned forward slightly, the small gesture commanding the attention of every man in the room. His intense focus on me pierced my chest like a blade, but I didn't flinch. An approving smile ghosted around his mouth as he addressed me directly.

"George Crawford is a dirty agent," he informed me, elaborating on the limited information I already had. "He's been working with my rivals, *Los Zetas*. They're trying to get a foothold in my territory, and Crawford is taking their bribes to keep the heat off them. Meanwhile, he's causing problems for me with his relentless investigations into my men, working off information the *Zetas* are feeding him. To his superiors, he's a model agent. They won't take it well when he's murdered by the Camorra. Especially when you have no business being in Mexico City."

"I don't intend to be caught," I replied coolly. "They won't know of our involvement. And you'll be kept out of it entirely."

He cocked his head at me. "The authorities will

suspect cartel involvement in his unfortunate disappearance."

"And they won't have any evidence to lead back to you," I assured him. "They won't be able to pin anything on you. Crawford won't cause you any more trouble."

He leaned back in his chair, considering me. "You don't strike me as a subtle man. But I'm trusting you to handle this delicately. Make sure this doesn't blow back on me. That would be a very unfortunate end to our friendship."

I offered him a grim nod. "I know how to make a man disappear. Don't worry about that."

"I trust Massimo with my life," Gian interjected.

"Despite his brutish appearance, he can handle a situation like this carefully and quietly," Enzo provided, backing me up with a bit of a jibe. Where his brother was all military rigidity and calm authority, Enzo was more suave: equally cool in the face of danger, but more charming than his aloof, unfeeling counterpart. They made an effective team, and my presence had always completed our intimidating trio.

With my imposing size, I looked the part of the dumb muscle to their wickedly clever, cold composure. But I'd been sure to educate myself despite my impoverished upbringing, a value instilled by my parents when I was a boy. I'd lost that innocence quickly and brutally at a young age, but I hadn't stopped reading everything I could get my hands on. Knowledge was as good a weapon as a knife, a truth that Enzo and Gian also understood.

"George Crawford is a dead man," I promised Duarte. "You don't have anything to worry about."

To his superiors, Crawford appeared to be a model agent, but he was getting rich by doing favors for a cartel. I would put an end to his promising career, and he'd never put his innocent fiancée at risk ever again.

The memory of Evelyn lying on that basement floor, broken and bleeding, flashed across my mind. It took effort to prevent my fists from clenching with renewed anger. That motherfucker, Crawford, was the reason she'd been targeted. He was just as responsible for her victimization as the men who'd kidnapped and beaten her.

Soon, he would be dead, and Evelyn would be safe from his corruption. I would make sure of it.

Chapter 5

Massimo

It hadn't been difficult to discover where George Crawford lived. The corrupt bastard kept his DEA friends close during the day, but it'd been easy enough to stalk him, hiding myself in crowds as he moved through the busy streets. Now, I concealed myself in shadows, closing in on my prey in the dead of night.

Their neighborhood was quiet at this time, the occasional car passing on the narrow street outside their building. The area wasn't particularly affluent, but it was fairly safe: an ideal location for a DEA agent and his fiancée to live. He couldn't possibly earn enough money to support her in the style she deserved, even taking dirty money from a cartel.

My lips curled in disdain. I couldn't end his miserable life soon enough.

The lights in their small ground floor apartment had gone out over two hours ago. They should be fast asleep by now.

Both of them: George and Evelyn, the innocent woman who had no involvement in my dark underworld. His criminal actions endangered her. That would've been reason enough for me to kill him, even without my promise to Stefano Duarte.

I approached their slightly derelict building with a nonchalant stride, as though I was returning to my own home after a night out. The neglect for the structure was apparent in the pockmarked brickwork and peeling paint on the window frames. Definitely not nice enough for a woman of Evelyn's caliber.

Still, it was good for me: the security for the apartment block would be dated and shoddy. Easy to bypass.

I doubted any neighbors would take particular notice of me at this hour, but I kept my baseball cap pulled low over my eyes just in case.

Once I reached their front door, I made quick, quiet work of picking the lock with practiced ease. I'd have to move silently if I didn't want to rouse George, who was likely to keep a weapon near his bed, especially after Evelyn had been targeted.

As it turned out, navigating their cramped, one bedroom apartment was almost laughably easy. It only took a few seconds to assess my surroundings and determine where George was located. In the moments I scanned the small living room, I noted that the space was immaculately tidy, and the framed artwork that dominated the walls probably brightened the space when the lights were on. Vaguely, I made out enlarged photographs: clearly art rather than simple mementos.

A woman's touch was obvious. Evelyn must've tried to make this dingy apartment a cozy home for them.

She was definitely too good for the selfish bastard.

I was quiet as a shadow as I moved through the darkened space, crossing the small living room in five strides before reaching the threshold of their bedroom. Soft illumination glowed through the closed curtains, the ever-present city lights impossible to shut out entirely. They caught on her platinum hair, the sheen drawing my eye to where she lay in the bed. Her fair complexion seemed to glow, like she was made of moonlight.

His slightly darker form shaped around her delicate body, an arm draped possessively over her waist.

His hand curved around her hip, locking her tightly in his embrace.

My muscles tensed with a pulse of rage, an echo of the fury that'd gripped my mind in that basement and caused me to murder Duarte's associates. This motherfucker dared to hold her when he was the reason she'd been kidnapped and brutalized. If not for me, she'd be dead now. Because of him and his selfish, greedy choices.

I took a step toward him, drawing my knife from the sheath at my belt. The wickedly sharp blade glinted in the dim lighting, flashing brighter than her moonlight hair.

My gaze flicked back to her fragile form, and my steps toward him halted. Her slender fingers were wrapped tightly around his forearm where it was braced at her waist, clinging to him in her sleep. A thick white bandage encircled her wrist, healing the wounds that'd been inflicted by her kidnappers' cruel restraints.

Despite my remembered rage, indecision immobilized me.

Even if I killed George quickly, I wouldn't be able to prevent his blood from marring her porcelain skin. She would wake up screaming, horrified at the violent death of the man who shared her bed.

My eyes narrowed on her hand where she clutched at him. She must love this two-faced monster. She held on to him for protection in her sleep, cuddling close to the man she'd pledged to marry. Her small diamond ring glittered through the darkened space, seeming to flash bright enough to sting my eyes.

She was innocent, but she loved this bastard. His murder would haunt her forever.

My own memories of brutal violence flickered through my mind in an unwelcome, macabre film reel. I'd lost my innocence on the day my parents had been butchered in front of me. I'd been too young to save them, too weak. And the last thing my mother had seen was my enemy's blood on my hands. The horror in her eyes before the light had left them was seared into my soul.

I took a jerky step back from the sleeping couple.

No, I couldn't do that to Evelyn. She'd suffered enough when Duarte's men had beaten her. I wouldn't add to the nightmares she'd carry for the rest of her life.

As though she sensed the danger lurking in the darkness, she stirred, tensing in Crawford's arms. My breath caught at her soft, fearful whimper, all my muscles locking up tight. If her nightmare roused him now, I'd have no choice but to act. He surely had a weapon stashed near his bed, and a moment of hesitation could cost my life.

But the selfish bastard didn't so much as stir at her distress.

Her shaky breath huffed through the silent bedroom, but she kept her eyes squeezed tightly shut. In the dim light, a single tear glittered on her luminous cheek as it slipped through her thick lashes.

Fuck.

She was awake, but she was hiding her residual fear from Crawford. She was likely reliving her trauma, and he slept peacefully beside her.

A reckless urge to wrap my arms around her and drag her away from him clawed at my mind, but I ruthlessly forced it down. I had to get the fuck out of here in case he did wake up.

Her next breath was a muffled sob.

I held my own breath and backed away, slipping into the shadows of the living room and out their apartment door before melting into the night.

I tasted copper on my tongue and realized I'd cut my cheek on my clenched teeth. That'd been too close. I never put myself at risk like that. In any other circumstance, I would've ended Crawford without a second thought. I'd survived this long because I was decisive and followed my most violent instincts without hesitation.

I shook my head sharply, as though I could toss the memory of her moonlight skin and glittering tear from my mind. Evelyn would be better off once her fiancé was dead.

I would just have to find a way to kill him so that she wouldn't be the one to find his dead body.

Chapter 6

Massimo

I hadn't seen Evelyn in a week. It would've made me edgy if it weren't for the glimpses of her silhouette through the drawn curtains when I stalked George back to his apartment at night.

I'd seen plenty of that slippery bastard over the last several days, but he was always surrounded by his fellow DEA agents. He must've gotten spooked by Evelyn's abduction, and he never went anywhere alone.

Not that he seemed to give a damn about her well-being. Three nights this week, he'd gone to the bar with his coworkers and left her isolated at home. Was she scared to leave the safety of their apartment? Did she still have nightmares and cry silently in his arms?

I remembered her moonlight glow, the starlight glimmer of the tear that had trailed down her cheek.

She'd been stunning even in the darkness, even in her distress.

She'd cried because of *him*. He didn't care if his corrupt actions endangered her.

I forced my jaw to unclench and refocused my wayward thoughts. Evelyn was a beautiful distraction I couldn't afford. I'd promised Duarte that I'd handle the threat to his organization, and I couldn't wait forever before eliminating the DEA agent.

Enzo and Gian had almost sealed our deal with Duarte and his Colombian partner, Adrián Rodríguez. Soon, they would return to Italy to set up the cocaine trafficking route on our end. I would remain here as Duarte's guest.

But in reality, I'd stay behind as leverage to ensure that my friends upheld their end of the bargain. The cartel bosses wouldn't ship their product to Europe without getting paid, so I would remain here until the transaction was complete. Once the infrastructure was in place, I could return to Naples, and my friends and I would be richer than we'd ever dreamed.

I just had to navigate the next few weeks with Duarte, and if I left George breathing for much longer, that wouldn't help solidify our new friendship. I had to follow through on my promise, or it would be my life on the line. My friends wouldn't be in Mexico to watch my back, and there would be little I could do against Duarte's small army of men. Over the last two decades, I'd learned to survive through honing my violent instincts, but I was only one man against many. Leaving George Crawford alive and well was bad for my health.

My fists clenched at my sides when the bastard finally emerged from his apartment building, stepping out into the bright morning light. I didn't see any of his fellow agents nearby. It was a Saturday, and he must have the day off. This might be my opportunity to get him alone in a quiet alley and...

Fuck.

Sunlight flashed over Evelyn's platinum hair as she followed him out onto the street, tucking her body close to his for protection. It seemed she was finally ready to venture out into the world after her ordeal, but she would still be jumpy from the violence she'd suffered.

I had to admire her bravery. After her isolation for the last week, I'd assumed she would become reclusive because of what she'd suffered.

The memory of her tears shining in the darkness played through my mind. I should've known she'd be resilient. She was strong enough to hide her distress from Crawford, probably to spare him from further worry about her wellbeing.

My eyes narrowed on him. The corrupt motherfucker didn't deserve a woman like her. But judging by the way she pressed her body close to his side, she loved the bastard.

She would probably weep when he died. But I could at least spare her the trauma of seeing his dead body.

Was the coward intentionally using her presence as a shield, since his fellow agents weren't around to watch his back?

I shook my head to clear the thoughts away.

His motives didn't matter. I had a job to do, and if I managed to find an opening, I'd kill him today. I just had to hope that Evelyn would be separated from him at some point.

I rolled the tension from my shoulders and began to follow them through the bustling city streets. Anger heated my chest as I watched them together: she clung to him, and he held her as though he had every right to own the innocent heart of this fragile woman. Physically, he was probably strong enough to defend her from most men, but he would be no match for me. I had at least thirty pounds of muscle on him, and I was accustomed to killing. He might be corrupt, but I doubted he'd ended as many lives as I had. I'd lost count over the long, bloody years.

I didn't lose sleep over it, and I wouldn't feel so much as a shred of remorse for killing this motherfucker. Especially if it meant saving Evelyn from him. She'd never be put in jeopardy because of his criminal activities ever again. I would guarantee it.

As I stalked them through the market, my attention remained fixed on Evelyn. I ignored the various vendors calling out to me, hawking their wares. I didn't give a shit about the fresh melons, handmade textiles, or fragrant flowers. The crowd was thick enough that I had difficulty keeping her in my line of sight, but I moved through the throng of people with practiced ease; this wasn't the first time I'd marked a target.

My gaze didn't waver from her. She hovered close enough to the bastard's side that I could tell myself that I was sticking to my task and hunting my prey.

But I kept watching her, my fascination deepening. She moved with graceful confidence, her shoulders straight and steps steady. Her head was held high, the sunlight shining on her platinum hair like a halo. She didn't cower or cringe in the aftermath of her ordeal, even though this was her first time venturing back outside.

Did she find that inner strength because *he* was with her? Did she think he would protect her if she was threatened again?

My teeth snapped, cutting the inside of my cheek. The way she looked to him to keep her safe made my blood boil, and the red haze of my rage hovered at the edges of my mind. The sight of her small hand clasped possessively in his was almost enough to make me snap. I hadn't been this unstable since the night I'd killed her kidnappers. It wasn't like me to lose my shit, not unless my life was in danger. But now, I hovered on the edge of murderous violence.

Luckily for Crawford, she released his hand when they reached a produce stall. Some of the tension eased from my muscles, and I managed to calm my most feral urges. Watching her rather than my enemy soothed the beast inside me, preventing me from recklessly attacking the motherfucker.

As she reached for an apple, I noted the white flash of the bandage that encircled her wrist. A shadow of my rage tightened my fists. She was still recovering from what those bastards had done to her, what her piece of shit fiancé had allowed to happen to her.

I took a breath and forced my fists to unfurl, but my attention remained fixed on her. She moved with a dancer's grace. Even the way her slender fingers trailed over the produce was alluring, her touch gentle as she considered the fruit, hunting for the best apple in the bunch.

Unbidden, a memory I'd long suppressed stirred at the back of my mind. My mother had been graceful like that, beautiful and pure hearted despite the grubby neighborhood we'd lived in. She'd helped my father at the grocery store, tidying the space whenever she took me to visit him during one of his long shifts.

I shook my head sharply, dashing the memories away. That was a different lifetime; I'd been a different person back then, a sheltered, naïve child. Now, I understood how the world worked, and there was no room for grace or tenderness in my life.

And yet, I couldn't stop watching her. All my muscles coiled tight with the effort of remaining still; I craved to cross the distance between us so that I could touch her delicate hand and capture her attention.

I wanted to see what color her eyes were. I'd witnessed her glittering tears, but I'd never seen her eyes open. At this distance, I couldn't make out the finer details of her lovely face.

I crossed my arms over my chest as though that would force me to keep my hands to myself.

She turned her face toward Crawford, saying something that made the bastard nod stiffly, a disapproving frown pinching his features. Her shoulders slumped slightly, but she flashed him a bright smile and brushed a quick kiss over his cheek.

I bit back a growl and forced myself to remain still as a statue, watching as she walked away from the produce stall, brown bag of fruit in hand. He shadowed her, that fucking frown still fixed on his face.

Evelyn approached a man who was huddled in an alcove, a sign begging for money clutched in his hands. For a moment, contempt heated my blood. The man could change his life if he wanted to; he just wasn't willing to make the hard choices necessary to survive.

Something tightened at the center of my chest when I finally noticed the small child who was tucked close to the man's side, clothed in a dirty t-shirt and ripped jeans. Evelyn leaned down and offered them both a kind smile, extending the brown bag in offering. Hesitantly, the child reached out and took it from her. The man nodded in thanks and said something I couldn't hear over the buzz of the crowd. Her smile faltered slightly, twisting with sadness for the space of a heartbeat before she pulled it back in place.

Crawford wrapped his arm around her and steered her away, pulling her back into the market and away from the pathetic man who would rather beg than do whatever was necessary to provide for his child.

My emotions surged, making me feel oddly edgy. Evelyn's compassion touched something deep inside me—the remnants of the innocent boy who'd been raised in poverty. But at the same time, I loathed the memory of that weak, helpless child.

And I hated the dark memories of the day my innocence had died a brutal, agonizing death.

Gritting my teeth, I directed my hatred outward, choosing to blame the wretched beggar for his own misfortune and for neglecting his child.

And most of all, I hated George Crawford, the corrupt piece of shit who dared to touch innocent Evelyn with his dirty hands. The bastard held her like he was protecting her, when he was the reason that her life had been endangered. His ties to *Los Zetas* had gotten her kidnapped and beaten. She'd be dead if it weren't for me.

I'd been the one to save her. Not him.

And yet, she leaned into him for support. She brushed her lips over his in a tender kiss. Her dainty hand clasped his as though he was the most important person in her world.

Contempt and jealousy curled my lips in a sneer. I took a single step toward them before I could stop myself, wanting nothing more than to rip him away from her and end his miserable life.

My movement caught her attention, and her pale green eyes flashed to mine. Her clear, peridot gaze punched me, knocking the air from my lungs. I went utterly still, as though I'd spook the beautiful creature if I made a sudden move. Her features were sharply defined but delicate, almost elfin, and her lovely eyes were large, like a pretty doll. Everything about her physical appearance exuded fragile grace, but I'd seen her inner strength, her bravery.

I barely breathed as she stared at me, our gazes locked. She was several meters away from me, a flower stall separating us. But her stunning eyes hooked me like a lure, commanding my full attention.

Hunger gnawed at my gut, a keen desire I'd never experienced before. I wanted this woman. I wanted her innocence, her beauty, her quiet strength. Everything about her fascinated me, and I craved more of her attention. I couldn't have broken from her gaze even if I'd wanted to.

Chapter 7

Evelyn

Shockingly blue eyes met mine from across the market, captivating my attention. They were so pale that they were almost silver, practically glowing like a wolf's keen gaze. The man's stare punched my chest like an arrow, painfully intense. His entire demeanor radiated power and masculine hunger that should've scared me...but the thrill that raced through my body made my belly flip with trepidation that wasn't entirely fearful.

His face might've been carved by a master sculptor, hard planes softened by full, sensual lips. Stubble darkened his square jaw, giving him a rugged appeal that captivated me. The tilt of his chin was proud, bordering on arrogant. And his high cheekbones defined his strongly masculine features with stunning effect, making that arrogance warranted. He was tall and broad—even bigger than George.

George.

Guilt lanced my heart, and I quickly tore my eyes from the beautiful stranger.

I'd been ogling a man right in front of my fiancé.

Cautiously, I peeked up at George. I released a relieved breath when I found his attention fixed on a food truck menu, his attention caught by the scent of richly spiced street food. The man I loved hadn't caught me staring at someone else.

I forced a smile to hide the worst of the guilt that still made my heart twinge with every beat. I'd never looked at another man before.

Admittedly, I'd never seen a man as gorgeous as the dark stranger with the shining wolf's eyes. Any woman would've been captivated. I was only human.

But I loved George, and I'd never betray him, not even in thought.

Determined to distract myself, I fished my phone out of my purse and immediately opened the camera app.

George's disapproving sigh ghosted over my neck, but he didn't rebuke me.

I released another relieved breath and cast my gaze around the market, hunting for a good shot. Luckily, the alluring stranger had disappeared into the bustling crowd.

For a moment, I wished I could photograph him, to capture those stunning eyes. I wondered what finer details I would be able to see if I were closer to him. Did he have laugh lines around his eyes and mouth? Did his olive skin glow with a dewy light under the sun? Did strands of silver shine in his glossy black curls, showing signs of maturity?

The man would be stunning at any age, his features classically handsome and boldly masculine, despite the softness of his mouth. His lips were full, sensual. But there was nothing remotely soft about his powerful aura.

Would I be able to capture that power through the lens of my camera? Or would it elude me, impossible to fully convey in a still image?

I shoved the thoughts away, struggling to dispel the aching guilt that constricted my chest. Instead of searching for the alluring man, I focused my attention on the flower stall. The blooms were stunning, flashing every color of the rainbow in fragrant bouquets.

I lifted my phone and framed a shot, only somewhat satisfied with the close-up of the heart of a pale pink lily. The composition was good, but I could capture more vibrant images in macro focus with my Nikon camera.

George hadn't allowed me to bring it out with me. My photography hobby was a distraction, and my ordeal with the cartel had proven that I couldn't afford to indulge in my art. This moment with my phone would have to be enough to satisfy my artistic urges.

"Come on, Evie. That's enough." George plucked the phone from my hand before I could frame a second picture. "I'm hungry. Let's get something to eat."

"Okay," I agreed with a sunny smile. The corners of my lips barely twitched with strain.

I could endure this lifestyle for a few short years. I could bear the isolation at the apartment and live in George's protective shadow when I did venture out into the world. Eventually, he would get his promotion, and then we could truly start out lives together in Albuquerque. I could endure anything for him. He was my whole world, and I was utterly devoted to his happiness.

Glossy black curls caught my attention, and I turned my head to search for the man's stunning eyes before I could stop myself.

But it was just the vendor at the flower stall, a tall, clean-shaven man who was several years older than the handsome stranger who'd captivated my attention.

Guilt nipped at me again, and I forced all thoughts of him from my mind. I was totally devoted to George, and I wouldn't allow myself to betray him even in my own mind.

I tucked myself beneath his arm and followed him to the food truck. If my fiancé was hungry, I wouldn't dawdle and delay. His contentment meant everything to me, and I would never do anything to jeopardize that.

I resolved not to think of the stunning stranger with the striking eyes ever again.

Soft lips brushed over my cheek, a tender kiss that made my skin flush. Warmth flooded my body in a slow wave, undulating through me to reach my fingers and toes. A deeper heat gathered at my core, throbbing to the point of aching.

The world was hazy, and I strained to make out his perfect features. The high cheekbones and sharp jaw wavered, as though I was peering at him through a wall of water. But his stunning eyes pierced me nonetheless, the silvery glint cutting right into my heart. It pounded in time with the throb between my legs.

I tried to reach for him, but I couldn't move. A

soft whine of need caught in my throat, and his sensual lips twisted into an arrogant smirk.

He leaned into me, gliding toward me in slow motion. As he neared, I still couldn't quite make out the finer details of his face, but his eyes commanded my full focus.

Then those sensuous lips caressed mine, and heat surged through my body, turning my core molten. My tongue traced the shape of his soft mouth, and my sensitive nerve endings tingled with carnal awareness I'd never known before. I was hungry for more, desperate. The ache between my thighs tormented me, and I tried to press myself against his massive frame to seek some relief.

I remained stuck in place, unable to touch him. All I could do was submit to his scorching kiss, melting as he thoroughly claimed my mouth.

I'd never experienced anything like the decadent sensation of those beautiful lips caressing mine. No kiss had ever come close to this one.

Not even with George...

I jolted awake with a gasp, my stomach twisting with guilt. I glanced over at my fiancé, and relief washed through me when I realized I hadn't roused him. He'd slept peacefully beside me while I'd dreamed of another man, the stunning stranger I'd seen in the market.

My cheeks flamed, and I touched my fingertips to my lips, as though I could brush away the phantom tingle of the sensual kiss.

It was just a dream, I reasoned. It wasn't as though I'd been unfaithful.

Still, guilt gnawed at my gut, chasing away the last of the strange heat that'd filled my belly.

Chapter 8

Evelyn

I finally took the last sip of the beer I'd been nursing for over an hour. Even though George was just at the other end of the bar, I was still too jumpy to allow myself to get tipsy. I didn't intend to dull my wits, even if my social anxiety was strong enough to make my fingers tremble. I tightened them around the empty bottle and fixed my face in a practiced, serene expression.

George was networking with his colleagues, so I would give him space. I was just grateful to be out of the apartment. Even if I was still somehow apart from the people around me, at least I wasn't completely isolated. I was accustomed to being an outsider, a quiet observer. I'd never quite fit in anywhere—George was the only person who'd ever really understood and accepted me. He was the only man who'd bothered to break through the protective walls around my heart and earn my trust.

He might be distant at the moment while he focused on his career, but he was devoted to work for both of us, for the future he'd planned.

I took a quick breath and tried to dispel the worst of the tension from my shoulders. To prevent myself from picking at the label on my beer bottle, I set it down on the bar behind me and focused my attention on Sara, the vibrant, chatty woman who was married to one of George's coworkers. She gushed on about her steamy love life, completely oblivious to my distraction. I smiled and forced a giggle at an appropriate time in her salacious story.

In truth, I was deeply uncomfortable with the topic of conversation. My sex life with George was private. He wouldn't appreciate it if I casually gossiped about him.

"So, what about you?" she asked, brown eyes twinkling as they flicked to George and back to me. "Is your fiancé keeping you *satisfied*?" Her blonde curls swayed around her flushed cheeks as she let out a conspiratorial laugh. "He always seems so uptight. Is he a total control freak in the bedroom too?"

Heat flooded my entire body, and I was sure even my ears had gone pink with embarrassment.

The memory of my illicit dream arose, unbidden. For a moment, I remembered the caress of sensual lips on mine and the ache between my legs. I hadn't been able to move; all I'd been able to do was submit to his scorching kiss.

My body burned, and I wasn't sure if it was entirely from embarrassment over Sara's inappropriate question.

"George and I are very happy together," I hedged. "Sorry, I'll be right back." I waved in the direction of the restrooms and quickly made my escape before she could ask any more sordid questions.

It didn't matter that the fiery passion Sara described was utterly foreign to me. The stability and trust I had with George were far more precious to me than orgasms. I didn't need to one-up her inappropriate stories to prove my love for my fiancé.

I edged around the small crowd of people who were dancing to the vibrant music, swaying and twirling to the beat. The bar was a bit raucous, but I enjoyed observing the smiling revelers. I wished I had my camera with me to capture the moment, but I didn't dare so much as snap a shot with my phone. George was just across the room, surrounded by his fellow DEA agents. I was safe here, but I still wouldn't indulge in my art. George wouldn't approve.

"Hello, beautiful."

I jolted at the proximity of the masculine voice behind me. I whirled, ensuring my back was to the wall this time; no one would sneak up on me again.

I shook my head at the dark-haired man with the bushy black beard, arranging my features in a carefully pleasant expression. "I'm sorry," I replied in English. "I'm here with my fiancé."

If he thought I was a tourist who didn't speak Spanish, he might leave me alone.

"You're American?" He beamed at me as he replied in English, and my stomach sank. "I love your accent. Have a drink with me." He offered me one of the two bottles of beer he was holding.

I took half a step back, shaking my head again. "I really can't, but thanks, anyway."

Maybe he hadn't understood the part about my fiancé. I'd give him the benefit of the doubt and politely extricate myself from the awkward situation. I didn't want to cause a scene and distract George, not when he was working so hard to secure his promotion.

The man mirrored my step. "I bought this for you," he insisted, offering me the beer again. "Come on, just one drink."

My stomach dropped as another masculine form entered my personal space, far too close. He was massive, at least a foot taller than my five-foot-five frame. For a moment, all I could see was his back; broad shoulders completely blocked my view of the man who'd been nagging me.

I took a hasty step back, edging away from the menace that rolled off the man like a palpable force. When his profile came into view, my breath caught. His strong, stubble-shadowed jaw might've been carved from granite, and those sensual lips were peeled back in a contemptuous snarl. His muscular arm bulged and flexed with barely leashed violence as he reached out and plucked the beer bottle from the smaller man's hand.

Those fierce wolf's eyes fixed on his prey as he tipped the bottle back and took a long draw of beer. Then he gestured at the drink that'd been meant for me, still clutched in the other man's hand.

"That one is for you," he told the man who'd been harassing me. Something about his gravelly voice made my belly flip. His accented English was out of place, but I couldn't pause to process anything other than witnessing the tense scene that was unfolding before me.

He leaned in slightly, and the smaller man seemed

to shrink by a few inches. "I—I didn't realize she's with you," he stammered. "My mistake."

"Drink it," the stunning stranger commanded, voice rumbling like thunder. "Or don't you like the taste of whatever drug you put in her beer?"

My skin pebbled, the fine hairs on the back of my neck rising in response to the presence of a predator. I wasn't sure if the fearful reaction was because of the man who'd tried to slip me a roofie or an instinctive wariness of the dangerous, beautiful stranger who'd come to my rescue.

It was the same man I'd seen in the market over the weekend, the man I'd dreamed about; I was sure of it. Those eyes...

The sound of glass smashing on the hardwood floor jolted through my body, making me cringe. The drugged beer splashed my jeans and pooled around my worn sneakers.

My savior growled his frustration, white teeth flashing in a feral expression that made my insides quake.

"You think that will save you?" he seethed. "Now you'll have to taste broken glass too. I will make you lick it up like the dog you are."

My would-be assailant shuddered in revulsion and backed away, holding his hands up in a sign of surrender. "I'm sorry," he gasped out. "I'm leaving now."

The beautiful, terrifying stranger swelled with fury, his massive body tensing to attack.

"Wait!" I gasped, instinct driving me to stop the violence before I could think better of my actions. My fingers wrapped around my ferocious savior's corded forearm, as though I could somehow hold back this beast of a man.

Shock thrummed through me when he went still as a statue, his hard muscles bulging beneath my desperate touch. My skin sparkled with awareness, and electricity arced through my body: a giddy response. Somehow, I'd harnessed the attention of the powerful stranger, staying his hand before he could carry out his threat to brutalize the weaker man who'd tried to drug me.

Those silvery eyes flashed as he watched his enemy hastily retreat. When he'd almost made it to the door, I felt powerful muscles shift beneath my hand, and I knew my savior was about to snap and go after his prey.

"It's okay," I said quickly. "I'm okay."

It was all I could think to say to soothe his protective fury. I was grateful he'd come to my rescue, but I couldn't bear to witness the carnage of what he'd threatened to make the man do. After my ordeal with the cartel, the prospect of more violence made my blood run cold.

He rounded on me, and his intense gaze punched the air from my chest. Striations of golden fire threaded through his pale blue irises, making them burn like twin flames.

"Go back to your friend," he rumbled, a deep command that rolled through my body.

I finally placed his accent: Italian. What was he doing here in Mexico City? Was he a tourist? I'd seen him in the market, and now he'd showed up in the same bar as me.

It was strange, but not beyond reason that he might visit both locations; the bar was in the same neighborhood as the market. There were probably many people who frequented them, but I'd only taken notice of this particularly beautiful, imposing man.

He captured my full attention so completely that I didn't notice the small crowd that'd parted around us: people giving the broken glass and dangerous man a wide berth.

"Go on," he prompted when I didn't move.

He wrenched his arm away, and my fingers tingled in the seconds after he broke contact.

"Your fiancé is waiting for you." He said the last through gritted teeth, anvil-hard jaw tight.

I blinked. How did he know about George?

Oh. I'd told the creep who'd tried to drug me that I was here with my fiancé. My savior must've overheard.

"I..." I swallowed down the lump of guilt that suddenly clogged my throat. George was just across the bar, hidden by the crowd on the dance floor. I'd been staring at another man, touching him...

"Thank you," I murmured, turning quickly and scurrying away from his alluring, powerful presence.

I hurried back to George, allowing the revelers to form a barrier between me and the gorgeous stranger. Just before I reached my fiancé, I schooled my features into a pleasant smile. I didn't dare rush up to him and confess what'd just happened. Guilt still churned in my gut.

Besides, George would be upset if he learned that I'd been harassed. He'd warned me not to leave his sight, and I'd broken my promise.

I went to his side and brushed a kiss over his cheek: a silent, secret apology for my transgressions. He placed a warm hand on my lower back in acknowledgement, but he didn't break his conversation with his boss.

I hid my disquiet well. This social time was important to George, for our future. I had no business thinking about another man, no matter how remarkable his eyes were. No matter the fact that he'd defended me.

No matter that when we'd touched, I'd felt a physical connection I'd never known before.

I leaned closer into George's hand. I belonged to him and no one else.

Chapter 9

Massimo

My forearm still burned with her touch, as though the delicate beauty had branded me when she'd stayed my hand. She hadn't wanted me to make that fucker pay for trying to drug her. He'd intended to violate her, but she had saved him from my retribution.

She was gone now, returned to the safety of the crowd of DEA agents. Crawford might be a corrupt piece of shit—his selfish actions put her in danger of becoming collateral damage—but no one would dare to assault her while she was surrounded by law enforcement.

I took a moment to catch one more glimpse of her gleaming, white-blonde hair, ensuring that she was safely back with the group of agents. She brushed a kiss over that motherfucker's cheek, and the bastard all but ignored her.

She hadn't run up to him to tell him about the danger she'd been in. She didn't cry and throw herself into the false protection of his arms.

No, Evelyn was too strong for that. She would shoulder the burden of what'd just happened, and she wouldn't say a word of complaint. I'd seen her strength in her silent tears when she'd hidden her nightmare from him; she'd quietly snuggled into his embrace in the bed they shared. She hid her distress so that she wouldn't disturb *him.* In her own soft way, she was protective of the man she'd pledged to spend the rest of her life with. She might not be strong enough to defend him physically, but it was obvious that she protected his black heart.

I gnashed my teeth. That callous fucker didn't deserve her.

I would eliminate him from her life soon enough, but I wouldn't get an opening tonight. Not when she was by his side, and he was surrounded by feds.

There was an outlet for my rage, though: the man who'd tried to assault her. He couldn't have gotten far, and I was good at hunting down my enemies.

It didn't take long to find the predatory fucker. I'd

prevented him from victimizing Evelyn, but he hadn't given up for the night. He hadn't even bothered to slink more than two blocks away; I found him in the third dive bar I searched.

I hung back, allowing the increasingly drunken revelers on the dance floor to separate us. The bastard was too busy eyeing up the single women in the bar to take notice of me.

After a few minutes of assessing his prey, he knocked back his beer and drained the bottle. His hand shook slightly; he was probably still unnerved from our encounter. The coward needed liquid courage before he'd try to drug another innocent woman.

Apparently, he'd chugged enough beer to need a piss. I followed him down the short corridor to the dingy bathroom. Just before he could shut the door behind him, I threw my weight against it, knocking him off-balance. My knife was in my hand as I kicked the door closed, trapping him with me.

I didn't give him time to scream for help. My blade sliced across his throat, and hot blood sprayed my face. His dark eyes widened in shock, and he lifted a hand to the gaping wound, as though he could hold the blood inside his body. I gripped his shirt in my fists, holding him upright so he could see death staring him in the face.

"I should've made you scream for mercy," I growled down at him as his mouth opened and closed like a dying fish. "But that doesn't mean I can't make you suffer for the last moments of your miserable life."

I drove my knife deep into his gut and twisted. A wet, choking sound caught in his ruined throat, and the whites of his eyes flashed as they rolled with agony.

"You like making women feel powerless? Do you feel like a big man when you rape them while they're unconscious?" I seethed. "You'll never hurt an innocent woman ever again."

I ripped my blade from his stomach and slammed it between his legs. Even though he had no hope of survival, I relished the abject horror in his eyes at being gelded.

I leaned in close, baring my teeth at him like a feral animal. He'd tried to drug Evelyn. He'd wanted rape her.

He was dying far too quickly.

"You'll never touch her," I snarled, his blood cooling on my rage-hated cheeks.

I would do what was necessary to keep her safe. Crawford would never do this for her. He only cared about his own miserable life. He'd put her at risk for wealth and power.

And yet, she was engaged to him. She belonged to that bastard.

For now.

I drove my knife into my prey's failing heart and allowed myself to imagine it was George Crawford's lifeblood spilling over my hand. Soon, his eyes would turn glassy, and his features would go slack, his mouth dropping open in a silent, perpetual scream.

I stepped away from the dead man and allowed him to drop to the ground, discarded like garbage. Then, I crossed to the grubby sink and washed away the crimson that coated my face and hands.

Before I closed the bathroom door, I twisted the lock so that no one would be able to enter once I exited. They'd have to get the staff to unlock it, and by then, I'd be gone.

I strolled around the crowded dance floor and made my way out into the warm night air. No one screamed in alarm behind me. They wouldn't find his body for a few more minutes, at least.

I wound my way through the crowded streets, losing myself in the bustle of increasingly drunken people as the city came alive for late-night revelry. My heartbeats slowed from the rush of murderous adrenaline, and I walked with nonchalance that wouldn't attract any attention from passersby. I took a breath and further soothed the last of my roiling emotions.

Evelyn was safe. I'd protected her from one monster tonight.

Soon, I'd eliminate the other threat to her safety: George Crawford was a dead man.

Chapter 10

Evelyn

Pale blue eyes shot through with golden fire burned into my soul. Warmth bloomed beneath the surface of my skin, and those eyes trailed over every inch of my body, caressing me like the lick of a sensual flame. His full lips tilted in an arrogant smirk, as though he knew exactly how his intense gaze affected me; it made me acutely aware of his presence in a way I'd never experienced before.

Long fingers trailed along my collarbone, brushing my hair over my shoulder so he could explore the curve of my neck. He tested my racing pulse, and his white teeth flashed in a purely primal, wicked grin.

The effect was stunning, knocking the air from my chest. Electricity crackled along my skin, arcing between us to create a sizzling connection. Little sparks pinged over my bare flesh, the sensation almost too intense to bear.

An answering spark danced between my legs, and my core heated.

His fingers trailed lower, brushing the line of my sternum as he traced a lazy path down my body. My breasts felt full and achy, and my nipples peaked. They throbbed in time with my clit, desperate for his merciful touch.

He loomed over me, his wicked smile taunting as he caressed the curve of my breasts without touching me where I needed it most. I whined in need and arched toward his big hands, but he eluded me with a low chuckle. The slightly cruel sound rumbled through me, a vibration between my legs. My thighs grew slick: a strange, new sensation.

My cheeks flushed with embarrassment at my wanton reaction, but I couldn't break from his burning gaze. His nostrils flared, a predator catching my scent. His pupils dilated, darkening with desire that matched my own.

One hand continued teasing around my breasts, a maddening touch. His other lifted to cup my cheek, his thumb hooking below my jaw. He held me as though I was made of porcelain as he tipped my head back, so I was locked in his fiery stare.

The sheer masculine perfection of his sculpted face was nearly unbearable to behold, his proximity arousing me to the edge of pain. My entire body throbbed in time with my racing heart.

"Please..."

Was that my breathy plea? I didn't recognize my own voice in that sultry tone.

"Evelyn..."

I shuddered at the raw need imbued in that one word: my name rasped in his low, masculine rumble.

My lips parted to sigh his name in return, wanting to savor the shape of it on my tongue.

But no sound issued from my throat except for my heavy, panting breaths.

I didn't know his name.

I didn't know anything about this dark, beautiful stranger who held me with such aching tenderness, setting my body alight with the barest brush of his masterful hands.

Guilt turned my stomach, souring my lust.

My eyes snapped open, and I blinked several times as I struggled to adjust to reality. The familiar shadows of the cramped bedroom I shared with George coalesced around me.

George. My fiancé.

My insides twisted. I'd been dreaming about the

handsome stranger who'd saved me tonight, not the man I was supposed to marry.

And my thighs were still wet with the very real arousal I'd felt in my dirty dream: a sensation I'd never experienced when I had sex with George.

I took a breath and turned to face him, intending to snuggle into his sleeping form and reassure myself that I was right where I belonged: with the man I loved.

His pillow was cool beside me. I was alone in our bed.

"George?" I murmured. My voice hitched on his name, a shadow of guilt constricting my throat.

He didn't reply.

I rolled over and reached for my phone to check the time. It was still dark outside. Surely, he hadn't already left for work?

1:27 AM.

"George?" I called out for him, loud enough that he'd hear me if he was in the living room or kitchen.

No reply. The apartment was silent, the only sounds coming from the street outside. It was fairly quiet at this time, but the occasional car passed, and I could hear masculine voices in what sounded like an argument. The tone of one of the voices was familiar, even though I couldn't understand the words.

George was outside for some reason. Was one of his coworkers in trouble? I'd noticed that more than one of his fellow agents had been fairly tipsy when we'd left the bar, and they'd ordered more drinks as we'd said our goodbyes.

It was considerate of George to keep the conversation outside so that he wouldn't disturb me, but if someone needed help—a place to crash or even just a glass of water to sober up—they were welcome to come into our apartment.

I got out of bed and grabbed one of George's big shirts to slip on over my thin camisole. My nipples were still peaked from my illicit dream, and I needed to hide the evidence of my traitorous subconscious. I decided that my silky pink pajama shorts covered me enough to step outside for a moment and invite his coworkers in.

I'd left my sneakers by the door to the apartment, so I slipped them on quickly, not bothering to tie the laces properly before I hurried to join George.

The voices became clearer as I rushed down the short internal corridor toward the exit to the street outside. They were speaking in English, but I noted the familiar Spanish accent in the way some of the others' voices lilted.

Odd. Most of George's fellow agents were Americans here in Mexico City, on similar assignments.

I shook the moment of confusion away, recalling that he worked in tandem with local law enforcement. A couple of cops had been at the bar with us tonight. George hadn't introduced us, but they'd been part of the group.

"I want my money," I overheard as I exited the building.

That was George's voice, an angry snap that I always dreaded in an argument.

My steps slowed. If he was in the middle of something more heated than a drunken misunderstanding, maybe I shouldn't interfere. I hesitated. All I had to do was step around the corner to join them in the quieter alley, away from the traffic on the main road.

But it sounded like I might be very unwelcome.

And what money was George talking about? I knew he liked to make casual bets with his friends, but I couldn't imagine him being so angry about a few dollars.

"The boss isn't happy," a stranger's voice replied, cooler than George's heated tone. "You're not delivering on your end of the agreement."

"Your rivals almost killed my fiancée. If I'd tried to save her, they would've killed me too. You're lucky I'm still willing to work with you at all. I'm risking my neck to do you favors. You owe me."

My stomach churned as my thoughts slowed, sticky like honey. I couldn't process what he was saying.

"We don't owe you shit," another man spat.

"I arrested three of Duarte's men for you," George insisted, terse and impatient.

"That's just doing your fucking job with the feds," the first stranger bit out. "Your boss is still investigating us. Half a dozen of us were killed in a raid last week. Where were you then?"

"I was in the hospital with my fiancée," George growled. "I could've been in the ground if Duarte's men had managed to get to me too. I'm still willing to do business with you. We can still have a profitable relationship."

I choked as my throat constricted with horror, the meaning of his words finally sinking in. George was working with these men, these criminals. They were talking about the monsters who'd kidnapped and beaten me: their *rivals*. And George had known who took me all along. He'd said he needed me to tell him that information so that he could arrest the men responsible, but he knew they were Duarte's associates.

If I'd tried to save her, they would've killed me too.

Now, he was demanding money from these men. These cartel members, Duarte's rivals. Demanding a bribe.

I shook my head, as though I could toss away all knowledge of this awful conversation.

No. This wasn't right. I was misunderstanding. George was a good man. He must be working undercover.

He must be. The alternative was too terrible to bear.

I took a shaky step back, reeling. The shoelaces I hadn't bothered to tie properly tangled around my feet, and a shocked squeak escaped my tight chest as I fell.

A hulking stranger whipped around the corner, his eyes narrowing on me where I lay sprawled on the warm pavement. George appeared beside him, and a third man lurked at their backs.

My fiancé's dark blue eyes widened as he took me in, his mouth going slack with horror for a moment. Then, his lips pressed into a thin, disapproving line that I recognized all too well. My stomach sank at the sight of it, a familiar dread that accompanied his censure.

"You shouldn't be out here, Evie," he rebuked.

He didn't make a move to help me up; he simply glowered down at me where I lay on the ground.

I licked my dry lips, and my attention flicked to the two dangerous men who were half-hidden in the shadow of the alley.

"What's happening?" I asked in a fearful whisper. "Who are they?"

But I knew. I'd heard. They worked for a cartel. And George had said...

In one smooth, lethal motion, one of the cartel members trained a gun on my heart. It didn't have time to skip a beat before a massive shadow slammed into him. A gunshot cracked through the night air like a whip, and I tried to scramble back, instinctively seeking cover. My palms scraped on the concrete, but I didn't manage to shuffle more than a few inches before the shadowy form of a beastly man blocked my view, looming over me.

I couldn't force the necessary air into my chest to release a scream.

Sprinting footfalls slapped against the ground, making a quick retreat.

The shadow above me shifted, moving with swift, brutal grace. The man who'd turned the gun on me was no longer visible, but another gunshot rang out.

My protective shadow let out an animal snarl, and in the blink of an eye, he disappeared into the dark alley.

A choked sound of protest caught in my throat, and I reached out as though I could somehow stop him and drag him away from the danger.

A sharp scream emanated from the alley before it was cut short.

Another set of sprinting footsteps, and I caught a glimpse of a second shadowy form running away from the fight.

I tried to stand, but I couldn't seem to move; my muscles were locked up tight, frozen in place. For a few fleeting seconds, all I could hear was a tinny ringing in my ears and the heavy, sawing sound of my gasping breaths.

Deep in my bones, I knew who'd fought off the man who'd tried to kill me. I'd recognized that massive, shadowy form, even from behind. The streetlights had shined on the glossy black curls that I'd just been dreaming about.

I heaved out a relieved breath when he appeared at the mouth of the alley, stunning blue eyes piercing the darkness to find mine. My thoughts were scrambled, disjointed. Everything was too much to process: George's traitorous conversation, having a gun trained on my heart, and the swift, brutal fight that'd saved me.

George. Where was he?

The alley was silent behind my savior. Someone had screamed...

"George." I managed to squeak his name as I struggled to stand, but I couldn't get my shaking legs to support me.

My savior's eyes narrowed, his square jaw ticking. "He ran."

Before I could tumble back to the ground, strong arms closed around me, lifting me as though I weighed nothing. The scent of leather and amber enfolded me, and I found myself tucked close against his broad chest.

"What are you doing?" I gasped, but I didn't struggle. I trusted this dark stranger who'd just saved my life.

I couldn't untangle my thoughts to wonder how he was here at the right time. The vague notion that he might work with the DEA flitted around the edges of my mind—he had been at the bar, after all—but fear still drenched my senses, sapping my ability to think clearly.

"I'm getting you out of here," he rumbled in reply. "They might have friends nearby."

He carried me across the street in a few long, sure strides. A motorcycle waited at the curb, and he carefully set me down so that I was straddling the seat. A helmet lowered over my head.

I didn't protest. My heart still slammed against my ribcage, everything in me driving me to flight. My trembling limbs wouldn't cooperate; I couldn't run away. So, I allowed the stranger to help me. He'd protected me twice now. He'd jumped in front of a bullet for me.

He must work with law enforcement to be so cool-headed in the face of mortal danger. He would take me somewhere safe, probably the police station. George would meet us there. Maybe my instincts were wrong. He might be working undercover.

He ran, the stranger had said.

The sound of those retreating footsteps echoed through my mind, and I shook them away.

George must have pursued the man who'd fled the scene. He wouldn't just leave me when an armed criminal was threatening my life.

If I'd tried to save her, they would've killed me too.

The memory of his awful frown and the cold disapproval in his eyes filled my mind, the terrible moment playing over and over again in a sickening loop. The two men in the alley with him worked for the cartel. One of them had pulled a gun on me, and George had done nothing. I'd recognized his disapproving glower all too well from our tense arguments, but the man who'd so callously stood by while my life was in danger was a stranger to me.

My tangled thoughts consumed me, but my savior didn't seem afflicted by the same distractions. Once the helmet was secure, he quickly got on the bike, and it roared to life beneath us.

"Hold on to me," he barked over the sound of the growling engine.

My arms wrapped around him, and my fingers knotted in his soft cotton shirt. I molded my body tightly against his back, clinging to him like he was my lifeline. He tensed as I squeezed his ribs, and his chest rumbled on a low grunt. The half-feral sound was swallowed by the roar of the motorcycle as we sped off into the night.

We wound our way through the city, dodging traffic far too fast on the busier streets. I shut my eyes tight, but the dark stranger seemed calm and confident, his breathing only hitching slightly when we made a particularly jarring swerve. I could feel his heartbeat beneath my clutching hands, and it was strong and steady. The fear that was making my own heart work overtime didn't seem to affect him, even though he'd been the one to risk his life to save mine. He could've been shot when he'd thrown himself into the fight, knocking the gun aside so that the bullet missed me.

And George...

My fiancé hadn't tried to save me. Where was he now?

He ran.

I swallowed against the acid that burned my throat and tucked myself impossibly closer to my savior. He would take us to safety.

I leaned into the beautiful stranger, instinctively seeking his protection once again.

Chapter 11

Massimo

I stopped the bike in front of the high rise building that Duarte owned in the heart of Mexico City. His enemies wouldn't be able to touch her once I got her inside.

Rage still tightened my jaw, but otherwise, my body was on autopilot; this wasn't the first time I'd faced down an armed opponent and won. Under other circumstances, I'd be completely relaxed in the aftermath of the swift, brutal violence. But that motherfucker had tried to kill Evelyn. He would've shot her in cold blood, and her piece of shit fiancé hadn't lifted a finger to save her. Crawford definitely wouldn't have thrown himself in front of a bullet for her.

More proof that he wasn't worthy of her. I'd be doing her a favor when I eliminated him from her life.

I needed to get her inside—where Duarte's guards would ensure that no one dared to follow us.

Her slender fingers were knotted in my shirt, her arms locked tight around my torso. I placed my hands over hers and urged her to let go with a firm squeeze. Her chest heaved against my back, her breath stuttering. She must be confused and scared right now. I would protect the fragile little butterfly from further harm.

"Let go, *farfallina*," I urged, tugging her grasping fingers free from my shirt. She didn't fight me. "Good girl."

I got off the bike and removed the helmet from her blonde head. Her platinum hair shined under the streetlights: a beacon, a target.

I scooped her up in my arms and rushed her inside, releasing a relieved breath as soon as the bulletproof glass doors closed behind us. Two armed guards greeted me with familiar nods, not commenting on my precious cargo despite their curious looks. I tugged her closer to my chest, shooting them both a warning glower.

No one would touch her but me.

"Where are we?" she asked in a shaky whisper as I pressed the button to call the elevator.

"Somewhere safe."

Her brow furrowed. "Like a safe house?"

My muscles tensed for a moment, and I forced my arms to relax around her so that I wouldn't scare her with my strength.

She must think I was associated with law enforcement. I supposed that made some sort of sense, given my presence at the bar and in the alley outside her apartment just now. She must be trying to rationalize my behavior in her fear-addled mind.

All that mattered was that she saw me as her protector. As long as she didn't try to run away from me, I could keep her safe without scaring her. I would prevent her from leaving this building if I had to, but I preferred not to add to her terrible ordeal tonight.

"You're safe with me," I replied smoothly: the absolute truth.

The elevator ascended to the fifth floor, where my suite was located. Duarte was an excellent host, and he'd made sure to provide my friends and me with lavish accommodations while we worked out the finer details of our business arrangement. Evelyn would be safe and comfortable here.

My friends. Shit. I had no idea how Gian and Enzo would react to her presence. I hadn't told the brothers about my obsession with George Crawford's fiancée. They probably wouldn't like it.

Luckily, they weren't in the suite when I stepped inside, Evelyn still cradled in my arms.

They would return eventually and discover us together, but I couldn't worry about that now. She was all that mattered.

I didn't want to release her from my protective embrace, but she shifted against me, apparently uncomfortable that I was still holding her despite the fact that we were safe from imminent danger. Reluctantly, I set her down on her feet, but I couldn't bring myself to break contact. My hands skimmed her upper arms, steadying her as she found her balance on shaky legs. Her creamy skin was so soft against my rough callouses. It pebbled beneath my touch, and I wasn't sure if that was a lingering fear response, or if she was as viscerally affected by our physical connection as I was.

Her pale green eyes were wide on mine, long blonde lashes nearly brushing her brows. When we'd been at the bar earlier, she must've darkened them with mascara, but I found her lovely like this: pure and perfect. She glowed like some ethereal creature, a tempting angel I wanted to ravage.

I trailed my palms down the length of her slender arms, loving the feel of her delicate body. My fingers brushed over wet fabric at her side, and fear punched my chest. A red stain marred the oversized white t-shirt that swallowed her fragile frame.

Evelyn was injured. I'd been so focused on getting her away from Crawford that I hadn't stopped to check if she'd been hurt. The sight of blood soaking her side froze the breath in my lungs.

Without thinking, I fisted the cotton material in both hands and ripped it open, desperate to check the damage and do what I could to stop the bleeding.

She gasped and tried to step away from me. "What are you doing?"

I palmed the smaller crimson patch on her pale pink camisole she wore under the t-shirt. She didn't cry out in pain when I applied pressure to the wound.

In fact, there was no wound.

It was my own side that burned, a familiar discomfort. It wasn't the first time I'd been grazed by a bullet.

She was covered in my blood. It must've soaked her shirt while she clung to me on the bike.

I grunted a curse and pressed a hand to my ribs, hissing out a pained breath at the contact. My palm was painted red when I lifted it for confirmation: I'd definitely been hit when I'd jumped in front of that bullet for her.

"Oh my god!" she exclaimed, her pale cheeks going porcelain white as she stared at the blood on my hand.

It wasn't visible on my black shirt, and the tear from the graze must've been hidden by the folds of the soft fabric—it'd been rumpled in the fight.

"You're hurt!" The sight of my blood clearly upset her.

"I'm fine, *farfallina*." I tried to reassure her, but her delicate features pinched with something close to panic.

"We have to get you to a hospital."

She grabbed my other hand, trying to tug me toward the door. I stood firm, not so much as swaying in her white-knuckled grip.

"You're staying right here," I admonished. "It's not safe for you out there."

She rounded on me, her lush lips pinched with determination. "Then I'll stay at the safe house without you. You need to see a doctor right now." Her chin lifted, and she seemed to grow a few inches taller as she tried to stare me down.

Despite the pain in my side, my lips curved. She was cute when she was being fierce, especially on my behalf. No one ever cared when I was hurt, not when the injury was so minor. My friends would've worried if I were bleeding out, but for this little graze, they'd tell me to sort myself out without complaint. They would do the same for themselves. We'd all learned how to patch ourselves up during the violent, thrilling years of our youth in Le Vele di Scampia, one of the poorest neighborhoods in Naples.

"I don't need a doctor. I can handle this myself," I told her, my voice sure and even. She was being brave, but I knew she was spooked from seeing the blood on me; she wouldn't be accustomed to the aftermath of violence like I was.

I didn't bother correcting her about the fact that we weren't at a safe house. I'd figure out how to deal with that particular misconception soon. For now, I needed to stop the bleeding that was upsetting her so much.

Her eyes narrowed, still fierce and defiant. "If you won't go to the hospital, at least call for a medic to come help you."

I took a moment to consider her. Despite her firm demeanor, she was still shaken from her ordeal. Her cheeks were too pale, and her pupils were dilated with fear.

Fear for me?

My chest warmed at the prospect.

"All right, *dolcezza*," I capitulated. She wouldn't be soothed until I was cleaned up, so I'd do what was necessary to calm her.

Duarte had a private physician, and I was sure our

host wouldn't begrudge me seeking treatment. He might have questions about how I'd been injured, but that was a worry for later. All that mattered now was erasing the strain from Evelyn's pinched features.

I retrieved my phone from my pocket and tapped out a quick text to Gian, explaining what I needed. His reply came within seconds.

> On our way.

My gut tightened. *Shit.*

Of course, my friends would think I was gravely injured since I'd asked them to call a doctor to come tend to me in our suite. Now, I'd have to deal with the brothers' questions, and I'd also have to navigate this situation with Evelyn. They wouldn't be happy that I'd brought her here, and they'd be even more displeased that I'd failed to kill Crawford.

I'd made a fucking mess tonight, and I had no idea how to clean it up.

All I knew was that Evelyn wasn't going anywhere. I wouldn't let her out of my sight until Crawford was dead, the threat to her eliminated.

I took another moment to study her. The ruined t-shirt that swallowed her delicate frame must belong to Crawford, smothering her in his scent. It irritated me even more than the sight of blood on her pure body.

My stomach soured with something like jealousy. I barely recognized the emotion, and it made me edgy.

I grasped her dainty hand in mine and led her toward the bedroom where I'd been staying for the last few weeks. Her footsteps faltered on the carpet, but I didn't slow to give her time to question me.

When we entered the massive bedroom, she sucked in a soft gasp and tried to dig in her heels. She tripped over those damned loose shoelaces.

I grasped her waist, steadying her before she could fall again, like she had on the concrete outside her apartment.

She didn't pull away from me, but she froze, her eyes wide on mine like a spooked doe.

"Are you hurt?" I asked. "You fell."

I took her hands in mine and gently lifted them so that I could study her palms. They were smudged with dirt where she'd tried to catch herself on the grubby sidewalk, but the scrapes weren't deep enough to have drawn blood.

"I'm fine," she replied in little more than a whisper. Her lovely eyes began to shine, and her throat worked as her emotions surged. A single tear rolled down her pale cheek, and I brushed it away.

"You're safe now," I promised. "I've got you."

"I don't understand…" Her chest heaved, but she forced down a sob by taking a deep breath. "What's happening? I don't even know your name."

"I'm Massimo," I replied, suddenly craving to hear the sound of my name in her breathy whisper. "I'm not going to let anyone hurt you ever again."

She swallowed hard and blinked away more tears, summoning up the quiet strength I'd witnessed in her on that night I'd broken into her apartment. I wanted to tell her that she didn't have to be strong around me; she could cry, and I would be more than happy to hold her.

But she was still wearing Crawford's shirt, and I wouldn't be able to shake the last of my rage until she took it off. My fingers itched with the urge to finish ripping it off her, but that would scare her even more.

I stepped away from her and quickly strode to the chest of drawers where I'd stashed my own clothes. I grabbed a soft black t-shirt that was a clean version of the blood-soaked shirt that covered my injured torso. Now that the adrenaline was fading, the burning in my side was becoming more insistent, and I was aware of how the wet cotton stuck to my skin. The graze probably wasn't deep enough to need stitches, but I was still bleeding sluggishly.

I draped my clean shirt over her shaking hands, which were still palms-up where I'd lifted them to inspect her for damage. She was frozen, posed like a doll, and her eyes were going glassy with shock.

I cupped her chilled cheeks in both hands, trying to imbue her with my warmth.

"Look at me," I commanded, a firm order.

She blinked, and her lovely eyes focused on mine once again.

"Good girl."

She released a shaky breath, and some of the tension eased from her slight body.

I stroked the lines of her cheekbones, leaving a crimson smear over her creamy complexion.

Shit.

My hand was still wet with blood where I'd pressed it against my side, and I'd marred her with the sign of violence.

I quickly brushed it away with my other thumb, but a pink flush still marked the spot where my blood had tainted her perfection.

I forced myself to pull away before I could imprint her with more signs of violence.

"Change out of that bloody shirt," I ordered, my voice holding a harsher rumble than I'd intended.

I needed her out of Crawford's shirt, all signs of his claim over her destroyed.

She blinked, her expression slightly bewildered, like a lost child.

"Now," I prompted, crossing my arms over my chest to prevent myself from tearing it off her.

Her hands trembled slightly as she tugged his ruined shirt from her body, revealing her modest curves that were barely concealed by the fitted pink camisole. Somehow, I forced my gaze to remain steady on hers rather than studying her feminine form; now wasn't the time to devour her with my hungry gaze.

She dropped the bloody shirt to the floor, and I kicked it farther away. I'd burn the damn thing later if I could.

To prevent myself from helping her, I kept my arms tucked tight to my chest while she tugged my shirt on over her blonde head. She was still shaking, but I worried I would spook her if I invaded her personal space when she was in such a vulnerable state. I never wanted Evelyn to fear me.

I enjoyed seeing myself as her protector far too much.

"Massimo!" Gian's voice boomed out from the sitting room as my friend burst into the suite.

I muttered a curse in Italian, and Evelyn blinked

up at me, confused by the change in language. I'd been speaking to her in English this whole time. Hopefully, she didn't understand Italian, so I would be able to talk to my friends without her understanding the conversation.

"*Stai bene?*" I asked if she was okay in Italian, testing her.

Her brow furrowed. "What?"

"Stay in here," I replied in English, satisfied that she couldn't understand. "I'm going to see the doctor now. I'll just be in the next room." I took a moment to gently squeeze her hand in reassurance. "No one will touch you here. You're with me now."

She swallowed and offered me a small, reluctant nod.

I didn't know how long I had until she figured out that I wasn't law enforcement, and this wasn't a safe house. But for now, my burning side was becoming a distraction, and I needed to soothe my friends' worries for my health.

My fingers lingered against hers as I slowly pulled away. She released a shuddering sigh when I broke contact, and she swayed toward me slightly.

Was it possible that she didn't want me to leave her?

"I'll be right back," I promised.

It took all my considerable willpower to turn away from her and stride out of the room. I straightened my shoulders, bracing myself to face Gian and Enzo's questions. My friends wouldn't be impressed by how I'd handled the situation with Crawford, and they'd wonder why I needed a doctor for such a minor wound.

I'd have to figure out how to tell them that I had taken Evelyn, and I didn't have any plans to let her go.

Chapter 12

Evelyn

"*Stai bene?*" Massimo's rumbled words played through my mind, not quite comprehensible. I was good with languages, but I'd never studied Italian. I wished I'd asked him what he'd meant, but I just stared dumbly as he slipped into the sitting room of the safe house suite.

My hands shook, so I clenched them into fists to hide the traumatic response. No one was around to witness my distress and be disturbed by it, but hiding the sign of unease was an ingrained response. I had a lifetime of practice at pretending I was okay, a skill I'd perfected during my six-year relationship with George. His happiness meant everything to me, and I didn't like to upset him.

George...

Two new, masculine voices joined Massimo's in the next room, speaking in rapid-fire Italian that I couldn't even begin to follow. Whatever they were saying, it was clear from their sharp tones that the atmosphere was tense.

My mind churned, struggling to process everything that'd happened since I'd awoken from my sordid dream, and my whole world had been turned upside down.

Massimo and his friends were Italian, not American or Mexican. Were they working with Interpol? I knew European agents sometimes collaborated with the DEA on international operations.

Massimo must work with George. It was the only scenario that made sense to explain his presence in the bar earlier this evening and at the clandestine meeting I'd overheard between George and the cartel members.

I want my money.

My heart stuttered at the memory of George's harsh demand. On the night I'd been kidnapped, I'd been targeted because of his involvement with the cartel. I'd been groped and beaten, and it would've been so much worse if the mysterious third man hadn't shown up and saved me.

That feral roar of rage that'd resounded through

the basement where I'd been held captive echoed through my mind. My entire body quaked.

That man had saved me, but he'd also killed the men who'd kidnapped me. George had told me that I'd been found in that basement with two dead men.

Is she innocent? my savior had asked in Spanish, one of the last things I could recall before I'd blacked out from pain.

He'd known my kidnappers.

And law enforcement agents didn't murder cartel members in cold blood.

Deep in my bones, I knew that the man who'd saved me that night wasn't a white knight. He was associated with the cartel somehow. He worked with *Duarte's* men. George had mentioned the drug lord's name during his heated argument in the alley.

If I'd tried to save her, they would've killed me too.

My thoughts tangled as my mind struggled to process all of the traumatic experiences I'd endured on that night in the basement and tonight, when I'd stared down the barrel of a gun.

My chest ached, as though it was on the verge of cracking open to release all of my inner turmoil on an anguished scream.

I sucked in a desperate breath to stave off my panic, and the scent of leather and amber suffused my senses.

I was wearing the beautiful stranger's shirt. The smell enfolded me, blotting out the scent of drying blood that made my camisole stick to my skin.

Massimo's blood.

He'd thrown himself in front of a bullet to save me.

And George...

He ran.

I heard the door to the suite open, and an unfamiliar man spoke in Spanish, a language I understood. "You were shot? Let me see."

It was the doctor, here to treat Massimo's wound.

I released a shaky breath and stepped toward the threshold to the sitting room, peering around the doorjamb to further assess my situation. Some instinct for self-preservation warned me not to boldly step into the room and join the strange men. The Italians had spoken in sharp, angry tones. I didn't know what I would be walking into, so I chose to linger in the privacy of the bedroom and take in whatever information I could.

The suite was surprisingly fancy, with ornate crown molding and bold crimson walls. Antique furniture with carved mahogany accents gave the space a sumptuous feel, and the highly polished, dark wood floor was cushioned by a large rug with an intricate red, navy, and cream design.

But it was the men in the room that commanded my full attention.

I got my first look at the two Italians who'd arrived first to interrogate Massimo. They were almost identical—clearly related. Both men were model-handsome and almost as imposing as my dark savior, even though Massimo was a few inches taller. He faced away from me, but I could clearly see the other two men in profile as they fixed him with twin glowers. The only discernible difference between them was their choice of hairstyle—one military short and the other in loose black waves that framed his granite face.

The clean-cut man barked something else in Italian, and Massimo rolled his shoulders as though shaking off irritation. Then, he grasped the hem of his shirt and tugged it over his head to reveal the gory wound at his side.

He was even more powerful than I'd realized, muscles rippling as he moved with shocking grace despite the pain he must be enduring. Blood coated his right side, and a darker gash scored his ribs.

The doctor went to work, inspecting and cleaning the damaged flesh. I swallowed down my nausea at the sight and focused on the Italians, who had resumed speaking to each other in their native language.

Amidst the indecipherable words, I caught on to one that they repeated several times: *Crawford.*

They did know George, then.

My heart skipped a beat. Did they know he was corrupt? Were they taking bribes from the cartel too?

Then Massimo spoke to the doctor in Spanish, and my whole world crumbled. "It's not serious. Barely a graze."

My stomach dropped. I recognized that oddly accented voice.

Is she innocent?

Massimo had been in that basement with me on the night of my terrible ordeal. He'd been the one to save me from the cartel.

He'd killed my kidnappers.

He'd murdered them to save me.

Now you'll have to taste broken glass too. I will make you lick it up like the dog you are.

His macabre threat to the man who'd tried to roofie me played through my mind. In that moment, I'd known he was dangerous, but I hadn't truly considered his capacity for such brutal violence.

And the way he'd handled himself when he'd jumped in front of the barrel of that gun to save me...

Someone had screamed in that alley, and Massimo had been the only man to emerge. In the aftermath of the fight, his heartbeat had been steady.

My chest convulsed, and an awful choking sound caught in my constricted throat. The bedroom spun around me, and I stumbled back, desperate to put distance between myself and the lethal man in the next room. The world tilted, and my knees hit the plush carpet.

My heart slammed against my ribcage with bruising force, and my lungs burned.

I couldn't breathe.

A tinny ringing pierced my eardrums, smothering the heaving sound of my failed breaths. They stuck in my tight throat, the air never reaching my oxygen-starved lungs.

"Evelyn." I recognized that accented voice. It was the first time he'd ever said my name.

How did he know my name?

Massimo wasn't an Interpol agent. He didn't work with George.

He shouldn't know my name.

Big hands reached for me—the same hands that'd scooped me up and carried me away from danger.

The hands that'd murdered the two men who'd kidnapped and brutalized me.

I tried to scramble away, releasing a whimper like a cornered animal.

His dark brows were dangerous slashes over his stunning wolf's eyes, and his full lips twisted in distaste.

"Please..." My mouth formed the desperate plea for mercy, but no sound came out.

Strong arms closed around me, dragging me close to his bare chest. He was massive, so much more powerful than I could ever hope to be. I'd never be capable of fighting him off, even if I were skilled in self-defense. As it was, George had always promised to keep me safe, so I'd focused on running to keep fit rather than building muscle.

Massimo's corded arms enfolded me, caging me against him in a careful but firm hold. One of his big hands lifted to the center of my chest, applying pressure over my racing heart.

"Breathe," he rumbled, a low command. His deep voice rolled through my body, compelling my obedience.

My chest loosened, and I managed to suck in a deep breath.

"That's it," he praised. "Another. Keep breathing."

I heaved in another ragged breath. My chest

convulsed, but I managed to take in the oxygen I so desperately needed. I forced down another.

One hand remained firmly on my chest, applying that grounding pressure against my heart as its erratic beats slowed to a more regular rhythm. His other hand brushed over my scalp, thick fingers trailing through my hair in a soothing motion.

"You're doing so well, *farfallina*," he said, warm and coaxing. "You're safe."

I tensed again, and he shushed me, cradling my face so that my cheek pressed against his chest. I inhaled the scent of leather and amber, and something deeper that was purely masculine and unique to Massimo. Every time my lungs expanded, I breathed him in. With his warm, sure hands soothing me, the scent became heady, and the world turned slightly surreal.

The room was no longer spinning, but it was fuzzy at the edges; my full focus was on *him*.

Two fingers curled beneath my chin, lifting my face to his. Those shining silver eyes stunned me, and my brain blanked for a few merciful seconds.

My next breath came easier. I could feel his steady heartbeat beneath my cheek where it was pressed against his chest, and my own heart slowed to match it.

"No one is going to hurt you," he said with the weight of an oath. "I've got you."

A shadow of fear flitted at the back of my mind, but I was too mesmerized by his intense gaze for true terror to stir. Or maybe I was simply wrung out from all the trauma I'd faced in the last few hours. Exhaustion rolled over me, making my entire body feel oddly heavy. I sagged in his arms, all instinct for fight or flight draining out of me.

"You don't work with George," I said, my voice strangely soft. I was so tired, and all that tethered me to reality were his arms and his silvery eyes, which seemed to hook my attention like a lure.

His lips pinched in a frown, but he maintained his gentle grip on my limp body. "No, I don't."

"This isn't a safe house."

"It's not." The admission was clipped, as though he was reluctant to say it. "But you are safe here."

"Who are you?" I asked on a little puff of air. My terror was still a mere flicker through my thoughts, kept at bay by his heavy hand over my heart.

"No one you should fear." His thumb caressed my chilled cheek, and I was tempted to lean into his warmth.

I barely resisted the urge. Something deep inside me knew this was wrong; Massimo was a dangerous man. I shouldn't find comfort in the hands that'd killed at least two men.

To save me.

"You were there," I whispered. "In that basement. You're the one who..." I trailed off, unable to put my roiling emotions into words. He'd killed for me, but he'd also saved my life.

"Yes," he replied, firm and unrepentant. "I will always protect you, Evelyn."

He'd protected me from the man who'd tried to roofie me in the bar.

He'd jumped in front of a bullet for me tonight.

But he was associated with the cartel somehow.

Maybe he was a good man. Maybe...

"Are you working undercover?" I asked, grasping at straws. "Is George?" I already knew the truth in my heart, but I had to ask, a tiny spark of hope still flickering in my chest.

His beautiful features twisted into a scowl. "Your *fiancé*," he spat the word like it was poison on his tongue, "isn't working undercover. He's corrupt, Evelyn. He's a dirty agent. The coward ran. He abandoned you. I saved you. I will always do what's necessary to protect you."

"You don't even know me," I protested, thoughts tangling as my heart was crushed beneath the weight of the awful truth.

I didn't understand why Massimo was so

committed to ensuring my safety if he didn't work with Interpol. If he wasn't one of the good guys, why would he care?

"I know you're innocent. I know you're a good woman. That's reason enough."

But how could he know that?

Is she innocent? he'd asked in that basement, during my nightmarish ordeal with the cartel.

He'd been in the market last weekend, watching me.

He'd been in the bar at precisely the right time to scare away that creep.

And he'd been in the alley tonight, as though he'd been waiting to rescue me.

My blood ran cold. "You've been stalking me."

His jaw ticked with something like irritation, and his arms tensed around me ever so slightly. "I've been stalking Crawford. He's working with *Los Zetas*. I'm just doing a favor for a friend." He shook his head, glossy black curls swaying around his sculpted face. "At least, that's how it started. I won't lie to you, Evelyn. I've been after Crawford, but you're the one I care about. You're in danger because of him—because of his negligence and selfishness. I'll do anything to keep you safe. He's not worthy of you."

My stomach churned at the implication. "And you are?" I shot back, fear finally surging to the fore along with my defiance. "You're a criminal. You work for the cartel, don't you? Let me go!"

I wriggled in his arms, but he didn't budge an inch. He simply held me, fixing me with a shining glower, until I stopped struggling. I crossed my arms over my chest and tipped my chin back, making my outrage apparent even though I couldn't physically fight him off.

"You're not going anywhere," he said. It was a decree, a vow.

I swallowed hard, my stomach dropping.

"I don't work for the cartel," he countered. "But Stefano Duarte is my friend. Your *fiancé*," his lip curled in disgust, "is working for his rivals. I'm doing Duarte a favor."

George's awful conversation in the alley played through my mind in a sickening loop.

"All he cares about is power and money," Massimo growled. "I know men like him. He would sacrifice anything for it, even you. I won't allow that to happen."

My insides quaked at his formidable frown, but I managed to hold my ground, my defiant stare clashing with his. No matter what was happening with George, the man who held me so gently had just admitted that he was friends with a drug lord.

"Let me go."

"No." It was a low, firm refusal. There was no room for negotiation in that hard tone. "It's not safe for you out there."

"I'm not safe in here!" I shot back, my voice a bit too high pitched. I took a quick breath to quell my mounting panic and hurried on. "You're a criminal. I don't know where you've brought me, but it's not a safe house. I want to leave. Now."

"Stefano Duarte owns this building," he replied coolly, completely unmoved by my outburst. "It would take a small army to penetrate his defenses. No one will get to you here."

My heart sank. Massimo had saved me, but he'd also kidnapped me. I hadn't known it when I'd willingly gotten on that motorcycle with him, but he'd managed to capture me with little effort.

All it took was risking his life to save yours, an unwelcome voice whispered in the back of my mind.

I ignored it. The cold, hard facts were that Massimo had been stalking me, and now he'd trapped me in a drug lord's fortress.

Looking up into his silver eyes, I saw a flash of possessiveness, a dark hunger as he studied my face. Massimo wanted me, and he had no intention of letting me go.

Chapter 13

Massimo

Evelyn's wide green eyes were fixed on mine, but her pupils weren't dilated with desire. Her pale cheeks and the lines of strain around her lush lips conveyed one terrible emotion: fear.

Evelyn was afraid of me.

My gut twisted.

I'd enjoyed seeing myself as her protector far too much. I should've known reality would ruin that eventually.

I straightened my shoulders, hardening my resolve. The fact was that George Crawford was a piece of shit, and she would be in danger as long as he was breathing. I would continue protecting her, whether she liked it or not.

Evelyn wasn't going anywhere.

But for now, I'd give her a little space to process her situation.

I became acutely aware of the faint pink smudge on her cheekbone where I'd wiped my blood away. There was more of my blood on her camisole, even though it was covered by my t-shirt.

Better mine than Crawford's.

That fucker had no claim over her. Not anymore.

She wriggled in my arms, and I reluctantly let her go. She reeled, as though she hadn't expected me to release her. I braced my hands around her waist, steadying her.

Her lovely eyes narrowed on me, and her chin tipped back in that defiant posture. She was brave, a quality I admired even as I craved to kiss the tension from her lips—until that impertinent expression melted from her delicate features. I wanted her soft and pliant in my arms, panting against my mouth with hungry lashes of her tongue.

I forced myself to let her go and take a step back. I crossed my arms over my chest to prevent myself from reaching for her again. She looked so damn fragile in my oversized shirt, her willowy frame appearing more delicate than ever.

Keeping her locked in a stern stare, I nodded in the direction of the ensuite. "Go get cleaned up. I'll be right here," I added, a reassurance and a warning. If Evelyn thought she had a chance of slipping away from me, she was mistaken. I would allow her out of my sight so that she could wash the blood off her, but I wouldn't stray far enough to give her an opportunity to run.

Not that she would get far. I could easily catch her, and I'd restrain her if I had to. I knew how to bind a woman to keep her exactly where I wanted her without inflicting pain.

The prospect of having Evelyn bound at my mercy made something dark stir in my chest. I took another step back, careful not to scare her even more. Any sign of carnal desire would terrify her, and I couldn't bear the fear that paled her complexion as she watched me warily.

"Go on," I prompted, my tone leaving no room for argument.

She stiffened with indignation, but she slowly backed away from me, not taking her eyes off me for one moment—as though I was a predator that might pounce if she allowed her focus to waver for even a heartbeat.

I didn't care for that, but I didn't ease my firm stance until she disappeared into the bathroom and shut the door between us. I heard the lock click into place, but that didn't concern me. No lock was strong enough to keep me out if I wanted to get to her.

For now, I would allow her privacy and space to gather her thoughts. Maybe some time alone would give her the chance to process the fact that Crawford had endangered and abandoned her.

It was past time for me to put that bastard in the ground.

"So, are you going to explain exactly what the fuck is going on?" Gian drawled from the threshold to the sitting room.

I turned and found the brothers facing me, both fixing me with twin disapproving frowns.

"Is that who I think it is?" Enzo asked, the scar that curved at the edge of his right cheekbone drawing deeper on a scowl. He grew his hair long to conceal it, but the mark was more prominent when he was pissed off. "She was talking about *George*. She's Crawford's fiancée. The one you saved that night you killed Duarte's men." He didn't finish with a question. It was a statement of fact: a condemnation.

"Why is she here?" Gian demanded. "And why isn't Crawford dead yet? Unless you're keeping her as bait." His frown deepened. "You're not usually this sloppy, Massimo."

"She's not bait," I snapped back. "But I am

keeping her. She's not going anywhere without me until Crawford is eliminated. She was almost shot tonight because of him."

Enzo hissed out a disapproving breath. We might all be perfectly happy with our lawless lifestyle, but none of us liked collateral damage. Innocent civilians were to be kept out of the line of fire. At least, that was the way we conducted our business in Naples.

"Send her back to the feds," Gian insisted. "You're not her babysitter. Let her be someone else's problem. We have enough of our own to be dealing with."

"Not happening," I refused. "I'm not sending her back to the DEA. Crawford will be able to get to her."

"She might want to be with him," Gian countered, infuriatingly calm and rational. "She's his fiancée, after all."

"She's *mine*." The fierce declaration left my chest on a snarl that I usually reserved for my enemies, not my closest friends.

Enzo blinked and took a step back. Gian looked like I'd punched him in the face.

A beat of heavy silence passed, and I forced my fists to unfurl where they'd clenched at my sides.

"I won't let her go," I declared, a hint of a growl still roughening my tone. "She's safest with me."

"Massimo, be reasonable." Gian maintained his

cool demeanor despite his shock at my aggressive outburst. "I get it. She's beautiful. But just because you want to fuck her—"

"Don't talk about her like that!" I thundered.

Enzo took another step away from me and placed a restraining hand on Gian, a warning to back off. The brothers weren't afraid of me; they cared about me. I was rarely this unstable, and Enzo knew my moods well enough to recognize that I was on the edge of violence. Back in that dirty alley, I'd ended the man who'd taken a shot at her, but it'd been too quick. I'd failed to kill Crawford too. I needed an outlet for my rage, and Enzo wasn't willing to allow his brother to draw my ire.

"Fine." Gian was smooth as ever, placating. "Keep her if you want. Just don't forget why we're here. We have to conclude our business with Duarte and his Colombian partner, Rodríguez. If we fail, we won't be able to take on the Boss back home." His dark green eyes glinted on the last: hatred and something more fervent, a burning need to wrest control from the old man who commanded our lives with the Camorra.

Most of the aggression drained out of me. "I won't fuck this up for you," I promised. "You know where my loyalties lie."

I would die for my friends. Gian and Enzo loathed

our boss, Cesare Salerno, a personal vendetta that went deeper than resentment of his casual cruelty. They'd made it their mission to overthrow the bastard and take everything he held dear.

We'd bided our time for years, and our work here in Mexico was the first clandestine move in our planned coup. Once the three of us controlled the lucrative new trafficking route into Europe, we'd have the global connections we needed to take on the boss. We would have powerful friends to back us up when the time came. Then we would be kings of our own domain, truly free for the first time in our lives.

It was everything we'd always dreamed of, going back to those early days of deprivation in Le Vele. It'd taken us over twenty years to get to this point; I wouldn't mess it up for us now that we were so close to attaining everything we'd ever wanted.

When it came to stalking Crawford, my obsession with Evelyn had proven to be a dangerous distraction. But now that I had her in my power, I wouldn't have to worry for her safety anymore. I could keep her close, and I would continue the work I'd started here in Mexico with my friends.

"I trust you," Gian finally replied. His posture remained relaxed, but his mouth still twisted in a frown. "But I'm worried for you, Massimo. Enzo and I are returning to Italy tomorrow. You have to stay here with Duarte while we arrange the payment on our end. We won't be around to watch your back."

Shit. I hadn't realized my friends would be leaving so soon. It would be up to me to play the role of charming Italian guest to solidify our alliance with the drug lord, a man who was notorious for his lavish parties. I would have to figure out how to navigate the social niceties with one of the most dangerous men in the world, and I'd have to manage it while keeping Evelyn close.

No matter the challenges, releasing her wasn't an option. Cartel violence had almost claimed her life twice now, and Crawford had done nothing to stop it. Evelyn wouldn't be safe as long as he was breathing.

"I'll be fine," I promised the brothers. "I can handle myself."

"We know you can," Enzo agreed. "But this isn't a situation you can fight your way out of. You almost attacked us over this woman. You can't lose your shit like that around Duarte's people. Especially when we won't be around to help you."

I offered him a grim nod, acknowledging my fuck-up. My possessiveness when it came to Evelyn clearly worried my friends, but now that I had her under my control, I'd be much calmer than I had been when Crawford still staked his claim over her.

I fixed Gian with a steady stare. The coup meant everything to both of them, but we all knew that Gian would be the one to take control of our organization when the time came. He was the cleverest of us, and his keen strategies had gotten us this far. I owed my fealty to him above all others.

"I will do everything in my power to seal this deal with the cartel," I vowed. "We've been planning this for years. I won't fail you now."

If I had to play the part of affable guest to Duarte's mercurial host, I would do it. Evelyn might try to put up a fuss, but she was no match for me. She'd be more amenable once she realized that I would take better care of her than Crawford ever could.

I resolved to lavish her with beautiful clothes and expensive gifts. I would prove to her how I could keep her safe and comfortable. And give her more pleasure than she'd ever known. Then, she wouldn't want to leave.

I wasn't the most subtle man compared to my wickedly smart friends, but I could be persuasive. Charming. Ruthless.

No matter how much she might protest at first, Evelyn would be mine.

Chapter 14

Evelyn

Hot water rained down on my bare skin, washing the dried blood from my side.

Massimo's blood. He'd risked his life to save mine.

I pumped out an excessive amount of body wash from the fixture on the wall and worked it into a lather. The soap slicked over my ribs and the curve of my waist, white bubbles turning to pink foam.

My stomach lurched, and I braced my hands against the tiled wall to steady myself. Taking a deep breath, I closed my eyes to focus on quelling my nausea.

I still felt weak and wrung-out from my panic attack, and I didn't have the energy for another one.

Exhaustion dragged at my limbs, but my fear-soaked senses were on high alert.

There was a criminal in the next room, separated from me only by a flimsy lock on the bathroom door. I wasn't foolish enough to think that would keep him out. I'd seen his intimidating physique when he'd taken off his shirt for the doctor to clean his wound. Massimo could easily break down the door to get to me.

Despite the heat of the shower, a shiver raced over my skin.

I was trapped in a drug lord's urban fortress, and I'd foolishly thought it was a safe house.

I will always protect you, Evelyn, Massimo had vowed. He'd proven himself three times already.

My gut twisted.

He'd proven it when he'd killed for me.

No matter what he said about keeping me safe, I knew the truth with crystal clarity: I was his captive.

On the night I'd been kidnapped by the cartel, they'd planned to use me as bait to get to George. Was that Massimo's intention too? He'd said that he was hunting my fiancé as a favor to Stefano Duarte.

I want my money. His angry words rang through my mind. *If I'd tried to save her, they would've killed me too.*

He'd always said that his work with the DEA meant everything to him. His desire to be a federal agent had been one of the things I admired most about him. It'd been his career aspiration ever since I'd first met him in our freshman year of college. He was supposed to be one of the good guys.

Even if George was corrupt, Massimo had to know that targeting a DEA agent was dangerous. From a criminal's perspective, there was nothing riskier than going after American law enforcement.

Maybe I could convince my captor that it wasn't worth the risk to target George. Then, he wouldn't need me as bait, either. He wouldn't dare hold me hostage if it wasn't advantageous for him. Not if that meant the DEA coming after him in full force.

I shivered again. Massimo had promised me that no one could get past Duarte's defenses. George had warned me about the manpower and weapons commanded by the cartels, and I didn't doubt that lives would be lost if agents tried to storm this building to get to me.

No one even knew I was here. How could the DEA find me when I'd so stupidly gotten on that motorcycle with Massimo, running straight into this trap?

I took another deep breath, struggling to slow my

whirring thoughts. If I was going to escape without risking others' lives, I would have to reason with Massimo.

Is she innocent? he'd asked in that basement. Right before he'd killed the men who'd kidnapped me.

No matter what kind of criminal he was, it seemed my dark savior had an undeniable code of honor. I could use that to my advantage. I might be able to talk my way out of this, and no one would have to get hurt.

Hardening my resolve, I opened my eyes and noted that all the blood had been washed from my skin. No signs of the violence that'd exploded in the alley marked my body.

I wasn't sure how long I'd lingered in the shower, sorting through my tangled thoughts. Trepidation nipped at me. Was Massimo a patient man? If he decided I'd been in here too long, he might decide to break that lock and come in here while I was still naked.

My fingers shook slightly as I quickly turned off the shower and stepped out into the opulent ensuite. A plush bathmat cushioned my feet, the heat from the tiles beneath ensuring that a chill didn't touch my toes. I grabbed a fluffy white towel and wrapped it around me, covering myself in case Massimo came bursting in.

Still, I felt far too exposed and vulnerable. I looked

at the pile of discarded clothes that I'd stripped off before I'd gotten in the shower. Dirt from where I'd fallen on the pavement smudged my silky pink pajama shorts, and putting on the blood-stained camisole was out of the question.

That left me with one option: Massimo's huge shirt. It was big enough to cover me almost down to my knees, and the loose garment would conceal the shape of my body.

I did my best to ignore the scent of leather and amber as I tugged the soft cotton over my head. Something had been rewired in my brain when he'd held me through my panic attack, and a tempting sense of comfort teased at my senses.

Before I could sort through the confusing emotions, a gentle knock on the bathroom door jolted through my body like a thunderclap. I yelped and tugged the shirt tightly around me, as though it would be enough to shield me from impending danger.

"Are you decent?" Massimo's deep voice was easily discernible through the closed door.

My reply stuck in my constricted throat, too tight from the surge of fear when he'd knocked.

"Answer me, Evelyn."

Was that anger that sharpened his tone? Or concern?

"Yes," I squeaked in reply, forcing out an answer before he chose to break down the door. I'd witnessed too much violence tonight, and I didn't think I could handle another outburst.

"Unlock the door." A firm order. "Now," he added when I hesitated.

I unstuck my feet from the warm tiled floor, moving to obey him. He would come in here, one way or another. I might as well take the smallest bit of control over my situation and unlock the door with my own hands.

As soon as the lock turned, he came in without waiting for an invitation. He stepped directly into my personal space, joining me in the bathroom. He was still shirtless, his muscular torso filling my vision with him so close to my body. My eyes caught on the small white bandage at his right side.

Massimo hadn't been seriously hurt. Some tension I'd been holding since he'd saved me released from my chest, and I huffed out a relieved breath. The sight of his blood and the knowledge that he'd bled *for me* had caused me more anxiety than I'd realized.

He's a criminal, I reminded myself. *He's holding you here against your will.*

Even so, I would've been tormented by guilt if he'd truly suffered for saving my life. No matter what else he might be, Massimo was a brave man. He'd jumped straight into the line of fire to protect me.

"It's my turn to get cleaned up," he announced.

My eyes lifted to his. How long had I been staring at his body, transfixed by the sight of his intimidating muscles? He could do anything he wanted to me, and I wouldn't be capable of resisting him.

His silver eyes shone with suspicion. "If I let you out of my sight, you're going to try to run."

It wasn't a question. My trepidation must be written all over my face—if I couldn't fight him off, flight was my only other option.

I struggled to smooth my expression to something meek and bewildered. "I won't."

His lips pinched, as though he'd bitten into something sour. "Don't lie to me, Evelyn."

Another lie teased at the tip of my tongue, but I swallowed it down. There was no hiding from his keen gaze.

"Let me leave," I pleaded instead. "I won't tell anyone about what happened tonight. You saved my life, and I owe you for that. I won't betray you to the cops, I swear."

He cocked his head at me. "You really mean that."

Again, it wasn't a question. Massimo was clearly

astute at reading people. Or maybe I was just too raw from my trauma to hide my emotions.

I nodded. "Let me go, and I won't say a word to anyone. Don't keep me as bait for George. Please, I—"

"Don't say his name," Massimo growled, eyes turning stormy. "I'm not keeping you as bait. You're here for your own protection. I'm not letting you out of my sight."

All of my muscles tensed, my body instinctively going on high alert. But before I could even think about evading him, his strong arms closed around me. Once again, I found myself cradled against his hard chest. I tried not to notice the warmth of his bare skin and the way his dark, masculine hair tickled my cheek.

"What are you doing?" I asked, my voice shaking slightly. Despite my worry over the unknown, true fear didn't grip my psyche. His compelling scent suffused my senses like a calming drug, and his hold on my body was achingly gentle, despite his strength.

He carried me into the bedroom and set me down on the enormous mahogany, four-poster bed. My heart fluttered, unease stirring at the back of my mind despite the decadent softness of the sheets and the way the plush mattress cushioned my body. I was naked beneath Massimo's huge shirt, and we were alone in his bedroom. His big hands touched me as though he had every right, handling me with ease.

"I'm going to make sure you don't try anything foolish," he told me, tone firm. "I don't want to have to deal with Duarte's men if they catch you making an attempt to leave the building."

I swallowed hard. "I won't..." The protest died in my throat when his silver eyes flashed in warning.

I didn't dare lie and say I wouldn't try to escape the moment his back was turned. Staying here willingly wasn't an option, and I would do whatever I could to get out of this drug lord's fortress, away from the criminals who defended it.

"Stay," he commanded, giving my waist a light squeeze to impress his order upon me. Warmth pulsed from his hands through my belly, gathering between my legs.

Before I could process my reaction, he stepped away, quickly crossing to the chest of drawers on the other side of the room.

My stomach dropped when I saw the rope coiled around his fist, and I scrambled back, nearly falling off the mattress in my haste to put distance between myself and the predator prowling toward me.

He was on me before I could get to my feet, his

sure hands clasping my ankles and dragging me back to the center of the bed.

"This won't hurt," he said, completely calm and unaffected by my struggles. "Don't fight me."

His long fingers ensnared my wrists, pulling my arms behind my back. Rough hemp rope lashed around my forearms, binding them so that my wrists pressed together, my fingertips brushing my opposite elbows. The position wasn't uncomfortable; it didn't put any strain on my shoulders. But being immobilized and made helpless caused my panic to resurface.

He pressed his warm palm against the center of my chest, just like he'd done when he'd calmed my panic attack. His chest braced my back, his big arms enfolding me in a perverse hug from behind.

He wasn't done restraining me. I wriggled in his firm hold, but the rope wrapped around my chest, binding my arms close to my torso. It wasn't tight enough to cause me any discomfort, but an intense sense of vulnerability settled over me. I'd never been capable of fighting him, but now I'd lost any illusion of control.

He finished off the tie at my back, but he didn't release me. His arms caged me in, that reassuring hand still settled over my racing heart, preventing it from beating right out of my chest.

"Breathe, *dolcezza*," he urged, the low command rumbling over my neck. "You're not hurt. You're safe."

A slightly mad laugh bubbled from my chest, and I jerked against the restraints. The rope shifted around me, holding me firm without biting into my flesh.

"So, is this what you do to your enemies?" I accused. Massimo had pretended to be a white knight, but he was a criminal, a killer. He'd bound me with ruthless efficiency, even if he had been careful not to hurt me.

His lips ghosted over the shell of my ear as he murmured, "Believe me, *farfallina*. This isn't something I do with my enemies."

Heat flashed beneath the surface of my skin, and my cheeks warmed at the implication. The way he was holding me was tender. Intimate.

Before I could process my body's reaction to his nearness, he pulled away with a sigh.

"You have nothing to fear from me," he promised. "This is for your own good."

My maddened laugh was more giddy than bitter. I couldn't process what was happening to me. I should've been terrified that a strange man was tying me up on a bed with him while I wore nothing but his shirt.

But I'd been through too much tonight, and my

emotions were scrambled. Massimo had proven that he only wanted to protect me. Or maybe the prospect that my dark savior might violate me was simply too horrific for me to contemplate.

Within less than a minute, he'd bound my ankles together with a second length of rope, rendering me truly helpless. I'd be incapable of running now.

I couldn't do anything but wriggle in protest as he lifted me up again, carrying me back into the bathroom with him. He carefully laid me down in the tub, so that the curve of the jacuzzi cradled my body. It was an odd position with my arms pinned to my back, but it wasn't too uncomfortable.

"I'm going to take a shower," he informed me. "I'll just be a few minutes."

"This isn't necessary," I tugged halfheartedly against the rope, but I was so tired that I couldn't muster up much of a fight.

"I told you, I'm not letting you out of my sight. That means you're staying right where I want you. Don't pretend you wouldn't have tried to run away as soon as I gave you an opportunity."

I pressed my lips together, refusing to lie. It would be pointless, and it would only give him reason to rebuke me when he read the truth on my face: I would do anything to get away from him.

Still, terror didn't grip my mind, not like it should. The knowledge that I had to escape from this criminal's fortress was more rational than instinctive. I was too exhausted for my instincts to rule me, and the rope that bound me made struggling useless, anyway.

His big hand cupped my cheek, and my breath caught. He traced the line of my lower lip with his thumb, and my sensitive skin tingled at the tender contact.

"You're safe with me, Evelyn. I'll protect you. Let me."

"Let me go," I managed to whisper, but there was no fire behind my demand. He was resolute in his determination to keep me here, and there was currently nothing I could do to resist him.

His jaw ticked, and he slowly withdrew his touch from my face, long fingers lingering on my cheek as he pulled away. My skin sparked at the contact, the same sensation that'd pinged through me when I'd first touched him at the bar, holding him back from attacking the man who'd tried to roofie me.

I was too exhausted to contemplate the way my skin pebbled and the warmth that flashed through me. My brain blanked, too tired to continue worrying about my situation.

If Massimo wanted to hurt me, he would've done

it already. He'd had every opportunity to beat me into submission or violate me while I was bound and helpless.

Instead, he handled me with tenderness as he tugged the hem of his shirt down my thighs, ensuring I was covered to my knees. His fingertips barely brushed my sensitive skin as he did so, and more sparks danced beneath his heated touch.

When he'd ensured my modesty, he finally pulled away and got to his feet, all six and a half feet of him towering over me. I felt small and achingly vulnerable, but I still didn't experience a flicker of fear. The world had become surreal, my thoughts going quiet. There was nothing for me to do but lay where he'd positioned me and wait for him to get cleaned up.

His silver eyes burned into me, pinning me with his full focus as his hands went to his belt. He unbuckled it and freed the button on his jeans before my slow mind processed the fact that he was stripping right in front of me.

I sucked in a soft gasp and closed my eyes, my cheeks burning. I could still feel his gaze on me, like a physical caress on my pebbled skin.

"You're welcome to look, *farfallina*."

I pressed my lips together and swallowed a reply.

The unformed words caught in my throat, and I released a sound like a soft whimper.

My cheeks flamed hotter, and I squirmed in his ropes. The jacuzzi was cool against my flushed skin, making me acutely aware of the warmth that'd bloomed in my belly.

A low, hungry growl rumbled through the bathroom, but he didn't say anything more. The sound of spraying water told me that he'd gotten in the shower.

My eyes opened a fraction, and I peeked at him through lowered lashes. The glass shower stall had already begun to steam up with the heat of the water, but I could still make out the imposing shape of his powerful body.

I sucked in a breath and squeezed my eyes shut again, reasoning to myself that I'd only been studying my surroundings to assess my situation. But there was nothing more I could do to try to escape now, and staring at Massimo's naked body wouldn't help me figure out how to get away from him. If anything, the reminder of his physical strength and how easily he could overpower me should make my stomach sink with despair.

But the warmth low in my belly didn't feel like despair.

I didn't dare contemplate it.

As I relaxed into the cool jacuzzi, the ropes cradled my body. My limbs were so heavy, and it was almost a relief to have the excuse that I couldn't try to run. I'd been through so much in the last few hours—multiple adrenaline dumps had left me weak and exhausted.

When the shower turned off, warm steam rolled over me. My eyelids were too heavy to lift, my body too tired to rouse any anxiety over what he might do next.

"Let's get you to bed, *dolcezza*." His low, sure tone blanketed me with comfort as his scent enfolded me.

Those corded arms cradled me once again, and I didn't bother fully waking to see where he was carrying me. I drifted somewhere on the edge of consciousness as he set me down on the soft mattress. His calloused hands brushed over my skin as he deftly freed the knots that bound me and slowly unwound the rope from my body. As he did so, his fingertips trailed along the slight indentations that the rope had left on my skin, and my nerve endings crackled with awareness.

I released a shuddering sigh, not quite waking at the strangely decadent sensation.

He laid my body down, and a plush pillow cushioned my head. A thick duvet settled over me just before his warm body shaped around mine, his hard chest pressing against my back. His fingers played through my hair, further lulling me into relaxation.

"You can sleep, Evelyn. No one will hurt you. I've got you."

With that promise, I drifted down into deep, dreamless sleep.

Chapter 15

Massimo

It was nearly two in the afternoon, and Evelyn was still sleeping. Unsurprising, considering it'd been dawn when I'd finally tucked her into bed. She'd stirred in her sleep a few times, her brow furrowing with an echo of the fear she'd faced. I'd held her through the tense moments, stroking her silky platinum hair until she slept peacefully once again.

Keeping one arm draped over her, I continued texting my friends with my phone in my other hand. Enzo and Gian were traveling back to Naples, so they could place the bribes we needed at Italian ports and arrange the payment to the cartel for their product.

They had a lot of work ahead of them, but my only job was to maintain a good relationship with Stefano Duarte until the deal was sealed. He'd invited me to one of his infamous parties tonight, and I couldn't refuse. I also wasn't willing to take my eyes off Evelyn. I'd have to figure out a way to take her as my guest.

And deter her from making a scene.

> I won't let you down.

I texted the promise to the encrypted group chat I shared with the brothers.

> I can handle Evelyn.

> How?

Gian shot back almost immediately.

> What do you think Duarte will say when he finds out you're holding Crawford's fiancée as a hostage in his home? You should have asked his permission before you kidnapped her and took her there.

I blew out a soft sigh, careful not to rouse Evelyn.

> She's not my hostage. I'm protecting her from Crawford. Duarte is the kind of man who will understand that. He didn't mind that I killed his men to save her.

Enzo was quick to remind me:

> Duarte won't like the fact that Crawford is still breathing.

My jaw clenched.

> I don't like it either. He'll be dead soon enough.

Once I took Evelyn in hand and ensured she wouldn't try to run from me, I would be free to resume my pursuit of Crawford. She seemed like a reasonable person; she'd endured horrors and hadn't broken down into hysterics. She'd been consumed by panic for a few terrible minutes—when she'd been afraid of *me*—but I'd managed to soothe her.

In her confusion, she might not realize the electric chemistry we shared, but I would use it to my advantage. She responded to my touch, and I would gladly take every opportunity to hold her.

> Have a safe flight.

I sent the final text and closed the messaging app. I didn't want to argue with my friends anymore. They needed to trust that I could navigate this situation, just as I trusted them to set up the infrastructure we needed in Europe.

I knew I was acting out of character, and that would worry them, especially when we were so close to attaining our goal. I'd never obsessed over a woman like this, and I definitely didn't hold them captive, no matter how dark my sexual games could become.

My connections with women were meant to be hedonistic and fleeting—fulfilling my most savage needs without the headache of emotional attachment. I was too busy with my work to indulge in long term distractions. Ensuring my security, power, and wealth was more important than a relationship. And my devotion to my friends' mission far outweighed my nonexistent interest in romance.

But Evelyn was different. The innocent beauty looked at me as her protector. No one ever looked at me like that. The feeling was new and addictive, and I craved more.

I reached for my phone again and tapped out a message to Duarte's staff, requesting breakfast. Evelyn would be hungry when she woke up, and I couldn't allow her to sleep for much longer. I had to talk to her about attending Duarte's party tonight. I had to make sure she would behave for me.

A few decidedly wicked ways to enforce her obedience played through my mind, but I shut them down before they could fully form. She would be terrified if she woke up to my hard-on. It was difficult enough keeping my lust in check with her delectable body cuddled up against me, her feminine curves barely concealed by my oversized shirt.

The sight of it on her pleased me more than was probably healthy. But after seeing her in Crawford's bloodstained shirt, the visible sign that I'd staked my own claim over her filled me with savage satisfaction.

I stroked her soft cheek, tracing the tiny, light freckles that dusted her creamy complexion. "*Farfallina*," I murmured, rousing her gently. "It's time to wake up."

Her long, pale lashes fluttered, and her brow pinched with confusion. Those stunning peridot eyes peered up at me, and I watched as reality darkened her lovely gaze. She was remembering where she was, what had happened to her last night.

I flexed my arm around her, tugging her closer in a reassuring embrace. "You're safe, *dolcezza*."

Her eyes began to shine, and she blinked quickly to hold back her tears. I cupped her cheek in my hand, grounding her to me.

"It's okay," I murmured. "You can cry. You don't have to hold back around me."

She'd hidden her distress from Crawford, protecting him from worry with her quiet strength.

But I was strong enough for both of us, and she didn't have to bear that kind of burden now that she was with me.

She blinked again and swallowed hard as she edged away from me. "Let me go."

I didn't budge an inch. It took no effort at all to keep her pinned to my side, trapped in my arms.

"I've got you," I soothed, brushing my fingers through her silken hair. She'd calmed when I'd petted her like this last night, but it didn't seem as effective now.

She squirmed. "Please." Her plea came out on a ragged whisper.

I couldn't bear the prospect that she might fear me, so I reluctantly released her. Maybe a little space would allow her to sort through her surging emotions.

She scooted away from me, clambering off the bed to put distance between us. Her eyes were wide on me, her gaze flicking over my bare chest before snapping back up to my face. She licked her lips and took a step back, putting more space between us.

Her pupils were dilated—with fear or desire?

I wanted to believe that she was aroused by the sight of my body, but she was undeniably shaken by everything she'd been through in the last twenty-four hours.

I sighed and nodded in the direction of the ensuite. "Everything you need is in the bathroom. Let me know if you want anything different from what I ordered."

Her toiletries, makeup, and clothes had been quietly delivered a few hours ago. Duarte had an efficient team on staff, and they hadn't asked any questions when I'd messaged them to request everything that Evelyn might need. I would make her comfortable here with me, and she would have no reason to want to leave.

She studied me for a moment longer, white teeth sinking into her pillowy lower lip.

Fuck, I wanted to taste her lips, to tame her tongue with mine.

My muscles flexed as I suppressed the need to close the distance between us and sweep her up in a scorching kiss. I still wasn't willing to scare her; Evelyn would never look at me with fear again.

Besides, I was skilled in seduction. I didn't need to frighten her to coax her into my bed. She would give herself to me soon enough.

"Go on," I prompted when she didn't immediately move to obey me.

We would have to work on that. I was accustomed

to having my orders followed without question or hesitation. If it weren't for her traumatic circumstances, her delayed compliance would've irritated me. As it was, I had more patience for her reticence. She'd been through a lot, and she needed a little time to process her new reality. Once she accepted that she belonged with me, she would be much happier and more amenable. I would give her everything she could possibly desire, and she would be eager to please me in return. Evelyn was tender-hearted and selfless; I'd seen those qualities during the days I'd been stalking her.

Soon, that devotion would be directed at me. She would be mine, body and soul.

"Breakfast will be here soon," I told her when she continued to linger. "You need to eat." I gestured toward the ensuite again. "You have fifteen minutes."

Her chin tilted in that same defiant posture she'd shown last night. It should've irritated me, but I was consumed by the nearly overwhelming urge to take her in my arms and kiss all the defiance from her fragile frame, until she melted against me. She would promise to obey me, promise me anything if I would just give her more pleasure. She might not realize it yet, but our chemistry was electric. She would love being my good girl.

"Now, Evelyn." My firm tone allowed no room for argument.

A light shiver raced over her, and her eyes dropped to the floor, as though forcibly breaking from the power of my steady stare. She moved stiffly as she walked the short distance to the bathroom, keeping her eyes averted from mine. Her posture remained defiant, but she complied, locking the door behind her.

I took a breath and struggled to master my lust. The small power play had stirred all of my most wicked instincts. I ached to touch her, to make her melt in my hands. I wanted her panting and pleading for more.

A knock on the door to the suite distracted me from my internal battle, cooling my mounting need for her. I pulled on a lightweight black robe and crossed into the sitting room, accepting the breakfast that waited outside on a cart. I thanked the server and wheeled the cart into the suite myself, ensuring that Evelyn and I had complete privacy.

I'd just finished setting the small dining table when I heard the bathroom door unlock.

"Come here, *farfallina*," I called out, another firm order. "It's time to eat."

I wouldn't allow her to neglect her needs. Evelyn was my responsibility now, and I would make sure that she was well cared for. She would never want for anything ever again.

She appeared at the threshold to the sitting room, her lovely eyes narrowed on me. "You can't just order me around like that."

I met her with a cool stare of my own, my brows raised expectantly. "You're hungry."

She crossed her arms over her chest. "I am not."

"I warned you not to lie to me, Evelyn," I said with the edge of a growl. I didn't tolerate dishonesty.

She huffed out a frustrated breath. "Fine. I'm hungry. But that doesn't mean I'll let you boss me around."

My mouth quirked in a crooked smile. She was cute when she was indignant.

I simply pulled out a chair for her and waited, keeping her locked in my expectant stare.

She glared at me and dug in her heels, lips pressing to a thin, angry line.

"You can sit down and eat your breakfast, or I can feed it to you while you sit on my lap." Even as I issued the ultimatum, the prospect of following through on my threat stirred my darkest carnal urges.

I was almost disappointed when she released an exasperated breath and strode toward the table. Her obedience should please me, but I craved to cuddle her close and feed her from my own hand. Now wasn't the time to hold her against her will, but I resolved to fulfil that particular fantasy soon.

She sat stiffly, her back ramrod straight.

"Good girl," I purred, and she bristled at the praise.

"I don't want to be here," she announced, keeping me fixed in that defiant glare. "I'm not behaving out of some desire to please you. I know I can't fight you. I can't outrun you. But you're making a mistake keeping me here. The DEA will figure out where I am, and—"

"Your *fiancé* isn't coming to save you," I snapped, a wave of ire surging to wash away my deviant pleasure.

She paled, but she didn't back down. "I know." She swallowed, her eyes shining with pain. "But I'm still an American citizen, and you're friendly with the cartel. You can't just kidnap me and expect to get away with it."

"I didn't kidnap you. You came with me willingly," I reminded her, not caring for the way she was twisting the facts.

"I want to leave," she insisted. "Are you going to let me go?"

"No," I replied flatly. "Don't ask again."

She rolled her shoulders, shrugging off the threat in my tone. "Then you're holding me captive, whether you kidnapped me or not. It won't make a difference to the American authorities."

"I don't give a fuck about the American feds," I growled. I probably should be more worried about them, but I was too obsessed with Evelyn to care. "No one will take you from me."

I hated the fear that shadowed her eyes and softened her defiant posture. I'd wanted to make her melt, not wilt. I would have to be careful not to crush my delicate little flower.

"I'll keep you safe," I promised, gentling my voice. I sat down beside her, so I wasn't looming over her anymore.

She tensed when I took her hand in mine, but she didn't try to pull away. Her fingers were chilled with fear, so I brushed my thumb over her knuckles to warm them.

"I can't let you go," I said, a confession and a promise. It was too late for her to leave me. Evelyn belonged to me. She would accept that, once I proved to her how I would take care of her in every way imaginable. "It's not safe for you out there. Crawford is still working for the DEA. If you go to the authorities for help, he will find you. And now that you know the truth about him, he won't let you live."

"You don't know that." Her voice hitched as she tried to deny the truth.

"He didn't lift a finger to protect you," I reminded her, keeping my voice gentle but firm. "He would've let his cartel friends shoot you to keep his secret safe."

She closed her eyes and turned her face away, as though hearing the truth in my words caused her physical pain.

"I don't want to be here," she whispered. "I don't want any of this."

I touched two fingers beneath her chin, directing her gaze to mine. "Look at me." The sheen of tears that brightened her eyes cut into my chest, but I kept my most volatile emotions off my face. Revealing the depth of my hatred for Crawford and the murderous rage I felt toward him for causing her this pain wouldn't soothe her. She needed me to be calm and composed, in control of the situation.

"The time for regret is over," I told her. "There's no going back. You know the truth about Crawford, and you know you're not safe with him. I will protect you with my life. Stay with me, Evelyn."

She didn't have a choice, but it would be easier for her if she could pretend. And I wouldn't have to worry about her trying to escape if she chose to stay in the gilded cage that I would build for her.

A single tear rolled down her cheek, spilling over despite her attempts to rein in her emotions. "I'm scared, Massimo."

Her admission hit me like a gut punch. It was the first time she'd ever said my name, and it'd wavered with fear.

But not fear of me. Not anymore.

Moving slowly so I wouldn't spook her, I lowered my face to hers. Her gorgeous eyes widened, and her lush lips parted on a sharp intake of breath.

"Don't be afraid, *farfallina*," I murmured against her mouth, allowing my low command to sink into her.

Her head tipped back, offering her lips to me. I caressed them with mine, the barest suggestion of the way I truly wanted to kiss her: to claim her with my tongue and teeth.

But I could be patient. Evelyn would come to me. She would welcome me to ravage her. She would beg and whimper my name.

As I thought about her delicious submission to my will, my cock stiffened. I couldn't deny my lustful reaction, but I wouldn't take it out on her. Controlling Evelyn gave me the strength I needed to control myself.

So, I teased her lips with mine and traced the shape of her mouth with a sweep of my tongue. Her breaths came faster, until we shared oxygen. Her arms twined around my shoulders, anchoring her to me. I allowed her to pull me closer, even though I could've resisted if I'd wanted to. Evelyn was so small and fragile, and I could easily overpower her.

I breathed her in to center myself, focusing on the light floral notes of her scent that mingled with my own. I wondered if she tasted as sweet as she smelled, and my lips firmed on hers, my hunger getting the better of me.

Soon, I told myself. I'd feast on her pussy soon enough. For now, learning the shape of her mouth and the way she gasped at light flicks of my tongue against hers was enough to temper my darkest urges.

She melted in my arms, and her kiss turned more frenzied, desperate. My lips curved in a satisfied smirk.

Evelyn was all mine.

Chapter 16

Evelyn

Massimo's lips were even softer than I'd dreamed, caressing mine in a skillful, seductive kiss. With every flick of his tongue, he stoked the heat gathering low in my belly. My breasts felt full and heavy, my nipples peaked to hard buds. I pressed my body closer to his hulking frame, wantonly seeking to stimulate them against his hard chest.

He hummed his approval and deepened the kiss, his tongue sweeping into my mouth in a confident, domineering stroke. My head tipped back farther, inviting his claim. His big hand cradled my nape, holding me in a careful but immovable grip. He kept me right where he wanted me and plundered my mouth, taming my tongue with his.

My core pulsed with arousal, an aching beat. I'd only ever felt this once before: during my illicit dream about the dark stranger who'd come to my rescue. I'd awoken, tormented by guilt for betraying George in my subconscious.

My stomach soured, and I broke the kiss. Massimo could've easily kept me locked in his firm embrace, but he allowed me to put distance between us.

Even as I felt sick with an echo of my misguided guilt, my body burned for him. I craved more of his fierce seduction, but that desire was wrong. Crazy.

"What's wrong, *farfallina*?" he murmured, silver eyes molten with worry and residual lust.

I shook my head. "I can't do this. It's just..." How could I put my roiling emotions into words? "It's too much."

I hated the guilt that churned in my gut. I had no reason to feel guilty, but I couldn't quite shake the awful feeling.

George. The man I'd thought I would marry. We'd planned to spend the rest of our lives together. He'd always wanted to be a DEA agent, a force for good in this world. And I'd intended to be his most ardent supporter, his devoted wife. I would've sacrificed anything for him.

I *had* sacrificed for him. I'd given up my job at the university. I'd isolated myself in that tiny apartment.

And even before then, I'd given up all career aspirations of my own to follow him to Mexico. I'd left my Fine Art degree collecting dust so that I could support his noble dreams.

But there was nothing noble about George. He'd sold his loyalties to a cartel. He'd stood by and watched as a man pulled a gun on me. I would be dead if Massimo hadn't saved me.

"You should take it off," Massimo growled, his dark brows drawn into harsh slashes over his glittering eyes.

"What?" I asked, following the direction of his glower.

I realized I'd been fiddling with my engagement ring, spinning the small diamond around my finger as anxiety ravaged my psyche.

I clenched my hand into a fist, instinctively refusing to take it off. I'd worn my ring ever since George had proposed two years ago, on the day we'd graduated from college. It'd been a constant sign of his pledge to love me forever, a love that no one else had ever offered me. Not even my parents.

A sense of utter loneliness crushed my heart.

Had any of it been real?

"You don't belong to him," Massimo insisted. "Take it off."

"I... It's not that simple," I protested.

If I took off the ring, I'd be accepting the awful reality of my current circumstances. I would have to fully acknowledge the depth of George's betrayal.

How long had he been corrupt? I remembered how fervently he'd expressed his desire to be an agent back when we were freshmen at college. Surely, he hadn't been lying to me then? Surely, every moment we'd shared couldn't have been a lie.

I didn't think my heart could bear the loss. Not only the loss of six wasted years with him, but also the loss of the future I'd envisioned for us in Albuquerque. My whole world was crumbling around me. The ring felt heavy on my finger, an anchor tethering me to sanity. If I took it off, I would be adrift, without direction or purpose. Supporting George's dreams had been my passion; his happiness had been my only concern in life. If my fiancé was content and fulfilled, that was enough to sustain me. Before meeting him, I'd been alone.

I couldn't endure that loneliness again: the isolation borne of callous indifference from the people who were supposed to love me unconditionally. My family had never given a damn about me. But George had. He'd loved me.

Hadn't he?

If I'd tried to save her, they would've killed me too.

Hot tears spilled down my cheeks, the floodgates opening. Maybe George had loved me once, but not anymore.

He would've left me for dead in that basement. He would've allowed me to be gunned down right in front of him without a word of protest.

My ring finger burned, as though the gold band was coated in acid. With a soft sob, I yanked the small diamond off my finger and tossed it away.

Massimo's arms closed around me, and I tucked my face close to his broad chest, breathing him in. He murmured a soothing stream of Italian while he tenderly stroked my hair. I couldn't understand the words, but the rumbling cadence lulled me into a sense of security. His powerful body enfolded mine, his imposing frame more than strong enough to protect me from harm. I felt small and achingly vulnerable, but I wasn't afraid. Not of him.

He held me while I cried, completely unruffled. His heartbeat was steady beneath my ear, the regular, deep pulse beating in a hypnotic rhythm. After a while, my breaths slowed to match his, and my own thundering heartbeat regulated. I sniffled, and he brushed the final tear from my damp cheek.

"You need to eat, *dolcezza*," he chided, and I suddenly realized that my stomach was aching with hunger.

I hadn't eaten since dinner last night, before I'd gone to the bar with George's colleagues. Before the man had tried to roofie me. Before I'd snuck out into the night and overheard George's traitorous conversation. Before...

"Eat," Massimo urged, pulling away from me so that I could finally face breakfast.

I took a breath and forced away all the dark memories, crushing my emotions into a tight ball and shoving them deep in my chest. I never allowed myself to fall apart the way I'd just wept in Massimo's arms. It'd been an awful moment of weakness, and I had to pull myself together.

I'd accepted the painful fact that George was corrupt, but I was far from resigned to my fate. Massimo wouldn't hurt me, and I had no doubt that he would do anything to protect me—he'd proven that so many times already.

But my dark savior was a criminal, no matter how tenderly he treated me. No matter how his touch set my body on fire. No matter how alluring his sensual lips were, tempting me to another kiss...

I tore my eyes from his handsome face and focused on the food. I had to keep my strength up and my wits about me. I was a captive in a drug lord's fortress. I would be a fool to give up on my freedom.

One way or another, I would get out of here, even if that meant leaving Massimo behind.

Chapter 17

EVELYN

"If you're finished, I'll show you what I ordered for you," Massimo said when I set down my fork. I hadn't spoken to him while I'd eaten, too consumed by my own conflicted thoughts about how I would escape. And how exposed I would be if I managed to run from my dark protector.

Somehow, I would get back to America, away from the cartels, away from George. Away from Massimo.

I'd kept my eyes downcast so that he wouldn't be able to read my thoughts—a skill that disconcerted me. I couldn't lie to him, so I couldn't risk him suspecting that I still planned to run at the first opportunity.

But now that he'd spoken to me, my eyes lifted to his. They glittered with anticipation, and his lips curved with a hint of pleasure. Whatever he'd purchased for me, the prospect of giving it to me excited him.

Unease stirred in my gut. In my experience, gifts always came with a price, a debt I couldn't pay.

I didn't want to owe Massimo anything.

"Whatever it is, I don't need it," I replied, shrugging off his offer.

His gaze trailed over my body in a lazy, indulgent appraisal. I became acutely aware that his thin cotton shirt was all that concealed my nakedness. His attention made warmth bloom beneath the surface of my skin, and my cheeks heated.

"Do you want to go to the party wearing only my shirt?" he rumbled. "Believe me, I wouldn't mind at all. That way, everyone will know you're mine."

His massive body seemed to swell, his powerful muscles flexing with something like pride.

I swallowed down the protest that teased at the tip of my tongue: I wasn't *his*.

But the other things he'd said were too important for me to argue over that misconception at the moment.

"What party?" I asked. "I don't want to meet any of your cartel friends." The prospect of being surrounded by criminals made a shadow of my fear flutter at the back of my mind. I did my best to ignore it; I couldn't afford the distraction of further emotional turmoil. Not if I was going to navigate this dangerous situation and somehow get free.

He took my hand in his, thick fingers brushing over my knuckles to soothe my mounting tension. "No one will touch you," he swore. "Duarte won't allow it. He knows I saved you from *Los Zetas* when they kidnapped you, and he approves."

"But Duarte wants you to...kill George," I stumbled over the word, my throat closing in horror at the prospect of his murder, no matter his corruption. "You said you're doing it as a favor."

He nodded, unruffled and unrepentant. "George is dirty. He dug his own grave when he sold his loyalty to the *Zetas*. You are innocent. Duarte appreciates the difference. He won't allow you to be harmed."

I pressed my lips together, considering my next words carefully. "I don't want to meet Duarte," I finally said. "He's a drug lord. That scares me, Massimo."

It wasn't a lie, and I allowed my dark protector to read the stark truth in my eyes. I wasn't accustomed to showing my more tumultuous emotions so openly, but if honesty would give me an advantage, I would use it.

He stroked my hair. "You don't need to be afraid, *farfallina*. You're with me." Before I could formulate another protest, he continued on. "This isn't optional. I have to attend Duarte's party to secure our alliance. My friends are counting on me, and I won't let them down."

"Your friends?" I remembered the two handsome Italian men who'd argued with him last night—the brothers. "Why can't they be the ones to go to the party?"

"They're on their way back to Naples. It's up to me to conclude our business here in Mexico."

My blood went cold. "And what *business* is that?" I demanded, daring him to admit to his criminal activities. It would be a good reminder for me too. The man who held me so tenderly was involved in organized crime, and I couldn't allow myself to forget it.

"Nothing you need to worry about," he replied, posture relaxed and completely unbothered. Whatever he was doing here in Mexico, Massimo didn't feel a shred of guilt over his lawless lifestyle.

I gaped at him. "You want to take me to a drug lord's party, and you think I shouldn't worry about what you're up to?"

He nodded. "There's no need for you to concern yourself with my business." He pressed a kiss to my forehead, and the shockingly intimate gesture made my mind blank for a moment. "You don't need to worry about anything. I'll take care of you, Evelyn."

Deep in my bones, I believed him. But that didn't mean I was okay with the situation.

"I don't want to go," I said, once again hoping the bald truth would sway him.

His lips ghosted over my cheek, his stubble lightly scraping my skin as he whispered in my ear, "I know what's best for you, *dolcezza*. I'm not letting you out of my sight, but I have to attend this party. That means you're coming with me, and you're going to behave." His teeth grazed my throat, a sensual threat. "I promise I will reward you after."

My belly fluttered, equal parts unease and arousal. "I don't want a reward." My protest was embarrassingly breathy when I should've sounded outright indignant. I was wary of any gifts that might make me indebted to him.

His low hum vibrated over my neck, sinking into my heated flesh. "You will. You'll be desperate for it by the time I'm finished with you."

Before I could demand to know what he was talking about, his teeth sank into my shoulder in a purely primal act of dominance. I cried out at the shock of pain, even as my core contracted in response. He kept me pinned in his ruthless bite and fisted my hair in one hand, anchoring me in place. My scalp lit up with little pinpricks of pain that turned into dancing sparks along my spine.

His other hand went to my breast, palming it through his soft shirt. My nipple was hard, straining against the fabric. He growled his approval, the sound rumbling all the way to my heated core. My thighs were slick with a shocking wash of arousal, an embarrassing sensation I'd never known before meeting Massimo. I squirmed, but he kept me captive in his savage bite, his tongue tracing soothing patterns on my skin even as pain radiated from my shoulder. It morphed into dark pleasure, sending lightning strikes straight to my sex.

Just when I thought I wouldn't be able to handle any more of the cruelly erotic sensations, he released me, and he pressed a tender kiss to the little indentations that he'd left in my skin.

"Now everyone will know you're mine." His voice was heavy with desire and a deep, wicked satisfaction.

The prospect of attending the drug lord's party with Massimo's bite mark on my neck caused anxiety to nip at me, but he quickly obliterated my budding concern by pinching my peaked nipple.

His lips crashed down on mine, devouring my sharp cry. Our first kiss had been a careful, slow seduction; this one was savage, rough with raw need. He claimed my mouth with tongue and teeth, kissing me so deeply that I could barely breathe. He consumed me, savoring the taste of my needy whimpers and soft gasps as he toyed with my breasts.

I'd never known my nipples could be so sensitive. Even through the barrier of his shirt, they tingled and throbbed beneath his deft fingers. His thumbs rubbed over the tight buds, teasing me until I became frenzied in my desperate need for more.

"Please," I panted against his lips. "Please, Massimo."

He groaned into my mouth and kissed me more deeply, almost feral. Abruptly, he tore his lips from mine, and I cried out at the loss. With one sweep of his powerful arm, he cleared the dining table. Plates smashed, and silverware clattered to the floor. I gasped in shock, but before I could ask what he was doing, his big hands sank into my hips. He lifted me as though I weighed nothing more than a doll, laying me out on the table before him.

I stared up at him where he loomed over me, his eyes burning flame blue as he studied my body. I studied him with equal intensity, my greedy gaze raking over his muscular chest and rippling abs where his robe had parted to reveal his impressive physique.

My tongue darted out to wet my lips, and he watched the sign of my desire with a low growl.

His hands fisted in the shirt that barely covered me, and the material tore like paper as he ripped it apart. Cool air washed over my heated skin, my body fully bared to him for the first time.

My hands flew to my chest and sex, instinctively covering myself. His growl roughened with warning, and his fingers encircled my wrists. He dragged my arms above my head, pinning them to the table.

"Never hide from me, *farfallina*," he rebuked.

I blew out a shaky sigh, modesty warring with my raging desire for this fierce, beautiful man. No one had ever looked at me in broad daylight like this; George had been my only sexual partner, and we always had sex with the lights off.

I took another breath and shoved the fleeting thought of my traitorous fiancé from my mind. As though he read my moment of disquiet, Massimo said something in Italian. I couldn't understand the words, but his cadence was low and soothing. Reverent.

Keeping my wrists pinned, he lowered his face to my chest, his eyes burning into mine. I watched with rapt fascination as his clever tongue flicked my nipple. Pleasure arced through me, and I barely recognized the wanton moan that issued from my chest.

His teeth grazed the hard bud on a wicked grin, an almost cruelly amused smile. Massimo was toying with me, indulging himself. His tongue explored the shape of my breasts as though he was memorizing my curves. With every deviant stroke, my belly coiled tighter with carnal need. My inner walls contracted, aching to be filled.

I squirmed beneath him, arching my back to seek his hot mouth on my nipples. His low chuckle rolled through my body, a vibration that reached deep into my core.

"Please..." I moaned again, lifting my hips in invitation.

All thoughts had been obliterated from my mind; I was consumed by erotic desperation. Massimo had become the center of my world, and all that mattered was his merciful touch on my aching sex.

His silver eyes were molten, searing my soul. "Say my name."

"Massimo," I whispered, barely finding the air to reply.

"Louder," he commanded, an almost fanatical light making his wolf's eyes gleam.

"Please, Massimo..."

"Tell me what you want." His calloused fingertips

teased my belly, just below my navel. "Beg me to touch your pretty pussy."

My clit throbbed in time with my racing heart, my desire for him so keen that it hurt. "Please touch me, Massimo."

He bared his teeth at me, a primal warning.

"Please touch my pussy, Massimo." Despite the embarrassment that flooded my cheeks with heat, I spoke clearly. I would do anything he said if he would grant me the release I so desperately needed. My body burned for him, for his masterful touch.

His dazzling, sharply satisfied grin hit me square in the chest. "Good girl." He stroked my cheek and gently squeezed my wrists with his other hand. "Stay."

He released me from the shackle of his long fingers, his touch trailing down the length of my arms, over the sides of my torso, down to my hips. He grasped me firmly and tugged me to the edge of the table, so that my toes brushed the floor. His grip shifted to my thighs, parting them as he dropped to his knees before me.

"What are you doing?" I asked in a breathy whisper.

"You were such a good girl asking for what you want," he rumbled, his breath hot on my slick folds. "I'm going to taste you."

My entire body flushed, and I squirmed in his hold. "You don't have to... No one has ever..." I trailed off, my mouth going dry at the feral hunger that sharpened his stunning features.

"This pussy is *mine*," he growled, staking his claim with a long swipe of his tongue over my swollen labia. He flicked my clit, and stars burst across my vision.

"I'm the only one to taste you," he declared, savage and possessive. "Your sweet cunt belongs to me. I could feast on you every day."

"Massimo..." I whimpered his name, tormented by embarrassment and desire. This was hedonistic, more decadent and deviant than any sex act I'd ever allowed myself.

But I'd never known my body could come alive like this. I'd never known that desire could be keen enough to hurt, relentless enough to drive me to the edge of madness.

He pressed a tender kiss directly over my clit, and a strangled cry tore from my chest as pleasure tormented me. My core contracted, and a fresh wash of arousal wet my inner thighs.

His animal snarl rumbled over my heated flesh, and I held my breath, bracing for the next surge of shocking ecstasy.

He pulled away, every line of his powerful body taut with strain.

Without thinking, I reached for him, my fingers tangling in his black curls to tug him closer to my needy clit.

Despite the tension in his jaw, he let out a cruel chuckle. "Greedy girl," he said, an admonishment and praise. "You'll get your reward later."

"What?" I asked on a little puff of air, bereft without his touch.

He grasped my wrists and directed my arms back to my sides. Then he lifted me off the table and set me down on my feet. I stared up at him, eyes wide and mouth agape. His thumb traced the line of my pouty lower lip, and my sensitive skin tingled with residual lust. I swayed toward him, desperate for more.

"Believe me," he rumbled. "This hurts me just as much as it hurts you. But you have to be good for me first. Behave tonight, and I'll make you come so hard that your voice is hoarse from screaming my name."

"Please... I can't..." It was too humiliating to tell him how much I ached for him, so I simply pressed my body against his, silently conveying the depth of my need.

"Soon, *dolcezza*," he promised.

As I molded my body to his, I felt his impressive

erection jerk against my belly. I gasped at his size and eased back slightly. Massimo was big *everywhere.* I was equally intimidated and intrigued, my body primed to accept him.

I shook my head to clear it and took another step back.

What was I doing? I'd almost been humping my captor. My protector. My dark, beautiful savior.

I swallowed hard and did my best to quell the lust that'd temporarily overtaken my sanity. It would be far too easy to become dangerously attached to Massimo. No one had ever looked at me the way he did: like I was the center of his universe. Like he would do anything to taste me again.

He licked his sensual lips in a lewd display, showing me just how hungry he was for more. My inner muscles fluttered at the sight of his raw need. This powerful, dangerous man had dropped to his knees before me. He'd pleasured me in a way no man had ever offered me.

Your sweet cunt belongs to me. I could feast on you every day. I shivered at the memory of his crass, possessive declaration.

"Go get ready for the party, *farfallina*," he ordered, nodding toward the bedroom. "I bought you everything you might need." His chest swelled with pride when he said it, as though providing for me pleased him.

But I knew such things always came with a price. He'd already made me malleable to his will by stoking my lust and leaving me wanting. Now, I'd be indebted to him, unable to repay him for whatever he'd bought for me. He'd asserted his control over me so easily, and there was nothing I could do about it.

I could choose to rail at him, but he'd proven that he was completely unaffected by my insistence that I wanted to go home. Arguing would get me nowhere, and being combative wasn't in my nature, anyway. I would rather quietly bide my time and assess my situation for any opportunities to escape.

One thing was for certain: as long as I was trapped in this suite with Massimo, I didn't have a hope of attaining my freedom.

Chapter 18

Evelyn

My anxiety increased with every passing second as we rode the elevator down to the mezzanine level of Duarte's personal nightclub. Massimo had told me the drug lord loved to party, and he had a clandestine club in his own building.

We wouldn't be venturing out into the open, beyond Duarte's defenses. I wouldn't get an opportunity to slip away from the cartel.

I wouldn't dare make a scene in front of a bunch of criminals, even if Massimo hadn't teased me to the edge of madness to ensure my compliance. My plan was to remain as small and unobtrusive as possible for the next few hours. I'd dealt with cartel members before, on the night the *Zetas* had kidnapped and beaten me. Massimo had said that Duarte wouldn't allow anyone to harm me, but I didn't intend to test that.

I edged closer to my dark protector, pressing my body close to his powerful form. His big hand spanned the small of my back, sending a pulse of warmth through my belly.

"You're all right, *dolcezza*. No one will dare to touch you." He dropped a kiss on the slightly tender spot on my shoulder, where I knew I bore the mark of his teeth. He'd chosen a daring red silk gown for me that left it on display, and I hadn't put up a fuss. If his claim protected me from being victimized by the cartel again, I would gladly let everyone know I was with Massimo.

The elevator doors slid open, revealing the VIP area of Duarte's club. Low music with a deep, sensual beat pulsed through the sleek space. In contrast to the sumptuous antique furniture and ornate crown molding in the suite upstairs, the club was thoroughly modern. A balcony allowed revelers to look down on the throngs partying on the ground level, and the opposite wall was lined with mirrors. Golden lights illuminated the empty dance floor—the guests were gathered near the polished ebony bar, socializing for the moment.

"Stay with me," Massimo commanded, steering me toward the small crowd with his hand firmly on my back.

I huffed an irritated breath at being ordered around, but I was too nervous to defy him. I had no intention of leaving his side, so there was no point in arguing.

My footsteps stalled slightly as we neared the other guests—the other criminals.

Massimo's thumb traced soothing circles over my bare skin that was exposed by the low back of the silky dress. A light shiver raced over me, and my sex pulsed despite my budding fear; it wasn't strong enough to quell the lingering desire from his wicked mouth on me. My body burned for him: heated with embarrassment and lust. I was keenly aware of the slickness on my inner thighs. Would everyone else be as adept at reading me as Massimo was? Would they know how hot and needy I was for my captor?

My cheeks burned, and I glanced over to find him smirking at me. He was far too smug and pleased with himself for reducing me to a panting mess.

I pursed my lips in irritation, holding in acerbic words. Challenging Massimo would definitely attract attention, and that was the last thing I wanted.

"Good girl." His thumb continued to trace lazy

patterns on my back, stoking the heat at my core despite my indignation. "You'll get your reward soon."

An outraged sound like a small growl caught in my throat. He just chuckled in response, as though he was thrilled at our game. He was enjoying playing with me.

I clung to my anger as we approached the cartel members. It was so much easier to bear than debilitating fear.

I glanced over at him again, and he winked at me.

Oh. Was he goading me on purpose? To distract me from feeling fear?

Between the puzzle of this gorgeous man and the lingering pulse between my legs, I was definitely distracted. I didn't have any room in my psyche for terror to take hold, not when my infuriating, alluring protector was toying with me.

"Massimo," a woman greeted warmly, "it's so good to see you. And your lovely guest."

My attention snapped from him to the stunning brunette who was striding toward us, the crowd of men parting for her. She moved with the grace of a jungle cat, her walk a smooth, confident saunter. The guests either respected or feared this woman, judging by the way none of them looked directly at her as she passed them by. She had a regal bearing about her, and I imagined she'd look quite natural wearing a crown.

Caramel eyes framed in thick, dark lashes assessed me, memorizing my face before dipping to the mark on my shoulder. Her rosebud mouth pinched in a small frown, and her eyes went cold when she turned them back on Massimo.

"Aren't you going to introduce us?" she asked pointedly.

Massimo's hand flexed against my back, but he offered her a smile that was dazzling enough to knock the air from my chest. "It's wonderful to see you, too, Carmen. Thank you for inviting us."

She did not appear charmed. A single dark brow arched, expectant.

"This is Evelyn," he introduced me. It seemed he didn't have a choice. Whoever Carmen was, she held power here, and Massimo was her guest.

"Evelyn," she repeated, my name heavy with condemnation. She eyed the mark on my neck again, and I barely resisted the urge to sweep my hair over my shoulder to cover it.

"It's good to meet you," she told me, her voice a touch warmer. Moving with smooth grace, she looped her arm through mine as though we were best friends. "Let me get you a drink. We have an excellent selection of mezcal."

She tugged me away from Massimo, but he simply

followed, as though his hand was attached to my back by a magnet.

"Not you, Massimo." She waved him away, flicking her fingers in an imperious gesture. "Stefano is eager to talk to you. Evelyn and I can get to know one another while you two catch up."

"I'm sure you'll want to be present for that," Massimo protested smoothly. "We can all have a drink together."

Carmen let out a melodic laugh that grated down my spine; there was no real humor in that laugh, only warning that her patience was wearing thin. "We'll join you soon enough. Please go entertain Stefano before he gets too bored. You don't know how difficult he can be when he's bored." She made a pained expression, dramatically put-upon. "It's past time for the party to get started, and he's been waiting for you."

My stomach flipped. I didn't want to be separated from my dark protector. I edged closer to him, and Carmen's keen eyes caught the small shift. The smile she offered me was kind, genuine.

"I just want to talk," she assured me. "No one here will harm you." She said it as though it was a guarantee, something within her power to promise.

Who was this woman? She obviously knew Massimo, and she'd mentioned Stefano Duarte twice.

She had to be associated with the cartel, but she was looking at me with soft concern.

My heart skipped a beat. This might be my opportunity to escape. Carmen clearly held sway here. If I got her on my side, she might let me leave. No one would have to get hurt, and I would be free to return to America, away from cartel violence.

"Okay," I agreed, stepping away from Massimo to join Carmen. His fingers brushed my back as I broke contact, as though he didn't want to let me go. "Let's talk."

"Carmen—" Massimo began, her name a low growl.

"Stefano is waiting." She cut him off breezily and steered me away from him, guiding me to a quieter corner where we could have a private conversation.

I glanced back at Massimo and found him scowling at Carmen. Another man stepped in front of him, creating a barrier between us with his body. Massimo was broader and taller, but he didn't toss the man out of his way to get to me. Instead, that dazzling smile slid back into place, and his focus shifted to address the slightly smaller man.

"Don't worry about Massimo," Carmen patted my hand in comfort before she extricated her arm from mine. She settled herself in a plush red leather armchair, making it appear like her own personal throne. Despite her powerful aura and regal poise, her sharply beautiful features softened when she looked at me.

"You're Evelyn Day," she said. It wasn't a question.

My mouth went dry. "How do you know my name?"

She pursed her lips, but her distaste didn't seem to be directed at me. "I make it my business to familiarize myself with my enemies and the people close to them. You're George Crawford's fiancée, aren't you?"

I swallowed hard. Maybe I'd made a terrible mistake in thinking that Carmen would be on my side.

"I didn't know anything about his involvement with *Los Zetas,*" I said quickly. Even now, admitting to the fact that George was corrupt sent pain knifing through my heart, but I ignored the discomfort. I had to keep my wits about me if I was going to navigate this situation.

"I believe you," she replied, placating. "My concern now isn't with Crawford; it's with Massimo." She glanced pointedly at the bite mark. "Is he mistreating you?" Her eyes stared at something I couldn't see, and all the warmth drained out of them. "I will not stand by and do nothing if there's an abusive man in my home."

Her home? She lived here—with Stefano. She was definitely associated with the cartel, even if she was currently concerned for my wellbeing.

When I didn't answer right away, her eyes narrowed, her gaze spearing him like daggers flung across the room.

"I don't care if it's an insult to the Camorra. I will kill him for violating you."

The Camorra. So, Massimo was with the mafia. I'd already known, but the confirmation made my blood run cold.

"I'm going to tell my husband to take our charming Italian guest to the basement. Stefano will make sure he regrets touching you before he finally allows him to die."

"What?" I gasped, horror chasing away my conflict over Massimo's criminal lifestyle. If Stefano was Carmen's husband, it was no wonder she wielded so much power here. She would order Massimo's execution, and the drug lord would carry out the sentence.

"No! Massimo didn't rape me. I..." The admission that I'd enjoyed every deviant moment of his erotic game stuck in my throat, too humiliating to utter. I'd willingly kissed my captor. I'd allowed him to touch me in ways no man ever had, and I'd begged for more. "He saved me," I said instead. "He's been protecting me."

Carmen's gaze snapped back to mine, those keen eyes peering into my soul. "I see," she said after a moment. "I understand that desire can be...complicated. If you're with him consensually, I won't say another word about it."

"Well, I wouldn't say I'm *with him*," I countered. "I mean, he saved me from George and *Los Zetas*. And he hasn't forced himself on me." My cheeks warmed, but I continued on, "But I don't want to be here. I told him I want to leave, and he won't let me go." Hope budded in my chest. Carmen cared about my wellbeing. She cared about my consent. "Will you help me?"

She cocked her head at me, long, wavy hair swaying around her lovely face. "What is it that you want? To be away from Massimo? You just said he's protecting you. And you've been with him willingly." She eyed the bite mark again, a pointed reminder of the fact that I'd eagerly kissed my captor and welcomed him to ravage me.

I breathed through my embarrassment and pleaded my case. "I just want to get back to Albuquerque. I can't stay here."

"Why?" she asked, a soft challenge.

I considered my next words carefully. She was Stefano Duarte's wife. I couldn't risk pissing her off. "I don't have anything to do with the cartels, and I don't want to. If you help me get out of here, I will leave Mexico City and go back home to America, where I belong."

Her jaw firmed. "You became associated with the cartels because of your fiancé's poor choices. I understand that isn't your fault, but that doesn't change the facts. You've been in my home. You've seen my face. You know who I am and what I do. I can't risk sending you back to the American authorities."

"I won't say a word to anyone, I swear." I tried to reason with her the way I'd reasoned with Massimo. "I would be dead if it weren't for Massimo. That's not a debt I can repay. I would never betray him, and there's no way I could tell the DEA about you without involving him. You have nothing to fear from me."

She laughed softly, genuinely amused. "I know I don't. I don't think you could hurt a fly. But I didn't get this far by taking stupid risks. I have an empire to run, and I don't intend to lose it. I've worked too hard to get to where I am, to be happy. I brought you over here to speak to you privately, so that I could find out if Massimo was abusing you. He's not. In your own words, he's protecting you from Crawford and *Los Zetas.* There's no need for me to be worried about you staying with him."

"I'm not *staying with him*," I said bluntly. "I'm his captive."

She shrugged. "Life is full of gray areas. The situation can be as difficult as you choose to make it. Believe me, I know."

"What do you mean?' I couldn't understand her cryptic words.

She eyed the man who'd blocked Massimo's path to us, her lips curving with unmistakable affection. "Let's just say that my relationship with Stefano had an unconventional start." She sighed and made a point of looking for a server. "Where is our mezcal? Honestly, you'd think they'd know to serve the women first. Come on." She grasped my hand and stood, tugging me toward the bar. "Let's get back to the men before Massimo decides to stop playing nice and drags you away from me."

Our conversation was clearly over. The cool queen was back, the concerned woman disappearing behind her regal mask. Carmen was satisfied that I wasn't in immediate danger, and she wouldn't do anything more to help me.

She hummed conspiratorially as we neared Massimo. "He is a big one, isn't he? Stay close to him. With his mark on your neck, no one will dare to breathe the same air as you. I would tell you to come talk to me if anyone bothers you, but I have a feeling they wouldn't be alive by the time you got to me." She sobered slightly, her coy smile firming to something more serious. "I've seen the way he looks at you. He would kill every man in this room to get to you. Massimo will keep you safe, Evelyn. That's what matters. He might even make you happy, if you let him."

I didn't have time to formulate a reply before we reached the men, and Massimo's big hand settled on the small of my back once again. Without thinking, I leaned into his possessive touch.

Chapter 19

Massimo

Duarte beamed at Evelyn, and the sharp edge to his grin made me tense with aggression. I wanted to snap at him not to look at her with that subtle threat in his black, shark's eyes, but he was my host. I couldn't protect her if I got myself killed for insulting the notoriously mercurial drug lord.

"It's so lovely to meet you, Evelyn." He addressed her warmly, as though he was genuinely delighted to make her acquaintance. Then his cold eyes cut to me. "Massimo has been very...*bold* in choosing to bring you as his guest. I was under the impression that you were engaged to someone else."

She stiffened at my side, and I traced a soothing

pattern on her lower back, trying to offer her quiet comfort.

I kept my own charming smile fixed in place. "Do you see a ring on her finger?" I asked blandly.

Duarte let out a soft hum. "Interesting. I must've been mistaken."

Carmen stepped close to him, and he draped a possessive arm around her waist.

"Don't interrogate them, darling." She brushed a kiss over his cheek. "Evelyn has chosen to be with Massimo."

My heart skipped a beat, and I couldn't stop myself from looking down at Evelyn. Her cheeks were flushed the prettiest shade of pink, and her eyes were downcast. I couldn't quite read her reaction to Carmen's declaration. Was Duarte's wife speaking the truth? What had the women talked about in their private conversation?

The prospect that Evelyn had indeed chosen me made my chest swell with pride. The stunning woman at my side belonged to me, and she'd acknowledged my claim publicly. She bore my mark on her neck, and she didn't try to conceal it.

"I didn't realize that the situation with her former fiancé had been handled," Duarte said, a genial but incisive remark. "It's good news if he's no longer in the picture." He wanted confirmation that Crawford was dead.

My smile twitched at the corners, but I quickly cleared away the sign of strain. "Evelyn is my primary concern at the moment." I allowed the weight of my loyalty to her to deepen my tone. She was my priority. Killing Crawford was an important secondary goal. She wouldn't be safe until he was dead, so his days were numbered.

"But I value our friendship, Stefano," I continued smoothly. "And I always keep my promises."

He offered me a small nod of acknowledgement, his displeasure evident in his glittering black stare. "Yes," he agreed, "I hope our friendship lasts a lifetime."

I heard the threat, loud and clear: my life wouldn't be very long if I didn't follow through on my promise and eliminate George Crawford.

"That's settled, then," Carmen announced, moving the conversation away from death threats: the epitome of a skilled hostess. "Aren't you going to invite our new friend on our trip tomorrow, darling?" she prompted Duarte. "I'd hate for him to miss the opportunity to meet Adrián."

Adrián Rodríguez was Duarte's Colombian partner. He worked with the Mexican drug lord to move their product from Colombia into his territory in America. My friendship with Duarte was important, but getting in with Rodríguez would secure my position here in the Americas. Gian, Enzo, and I would have a powerful friend in our corner when we finally made our move against our despotic boss back home.

"Where are we going?" I asked, accepting the invitation before Duarte could take it back.

"Colombia," he replied, keeping me fixed in his sharp stare. He still wasn't pleased by the situation with Crawford, but he wasn't ready to give up on our alliance over it. He had much to gain from our business deal too.

"We leave tomorrow morning." He glanced at Evelyn. "You are welcome to make yourself at home here while we're away."

"Evelyn goes where I go," I said immediately, too sharply. I took a quick breath and calmed my most savage urges. "I made a vow to protect her. I don't want her out of my sight."

Duarte's dark brows rose. "And you think she won't be safe in my home?" he drawled.

"Like I said, I always keep my promises," I replied coolly. This wasn't up for negotiation. Crawford was still in Mexico City. I wouldn't leave Evelyn here without me to guard her.

And I wouldn't be able to focus on my important business in Colombia if I didn't have her with me. I'd be consumed by thoughts of her. The depth of my obsession should've alarmed me, but with her slight body leaning into mine, I couldn't bring myself to care. She looked to me to shield her, and I was addicted to her trust in me.

"Do you want to come with us?" Carmen addressed Evelyn, allowing her the choice.

Part of me appreciated that she was offering Evelyn agency, but my irritation at the prospect of being parted from her far outweighed my flicker of respect. My delicate little butterfly wasn't leaving my side.

Before I could insist that she accompany me, Evelyn said, "I want to stay with Massimo."

Her soft declaration punched my heart like an arrow, and my feral desire for her surged.

Mine. She was all mine, and she knew it. She chose me.

It might be out of fear, but that notion didn't bother me. She'd made it clear that being in Stefano's home, the heart of his cartel, made her anxious. She didn't want to stay here without me.

She knew that I would keep her safe, and she didn't want to be parted from me.

That was enough to satisfy me for now. Her devotion would grow with time. She belonged to me, and there was no going back.

"Excellent," Carmen approved. "We'll all fly out on the jet tomorrow morning. Adrián is keen to meet you, Massimo."

"I'm looking forward to it," I replied absently, my attention fixed on Evelyn.

Her gaze was still downcast, her eyes averted. And that lovely flush colored her cheeks. I wanted to see that shade of pink while I feasted on her pussy again; I would make her cry out my name in ecstasy. Would her pert ass flush a matching shade beneath my hand? I craved to see it imprinted on her creamy flesh. She'd responded to the pain of my bite. Our chemistry was undeniable. She would come to accept the more deviant things I needed to do to her.

She was innocent, and I craved to corrupt her. I would teach her to enjoy my darker sexual games. Evelyn would love being mine.

"You two should enjoy the party," Carmen announced, a dismissal and a gift. My hunger for Evelyn must be plain on my face, and the cartel queen was giving me permission to be alone with my pretty little butterfly.

"Thank you." I managed a modicum of politeness

before I steered Evelyn away from the powerful, dangerous couple.

She'd been quiet for most of the conversation, and she was probably disconcerted by the interaction with Duarte. The man was intimidating, even though he played the part of impeccable host.

"Dance with me," I commanded, sweeping Evelyn into my arms.

She blinked up at me, slightly bewildered by the sudden turn of events. "I don't want to go to Colombia," she said, even as she began to sway to the beat, allowing me to lead her.

"I'll make sure you enjoy our little vacation," I promised, firming my hand on her waist.

She shivered and melted into me, submitting to the confident way I handled her willowy body.

"It's not a vacation," she protested, her peridot eyes glittering with frustration. "You can't just take control of my life like this. I want to go home, not farther away from America."

Your home is with me now. I kept the promise locked in my chest. She wasn't ready to hear it. Not yet.

"This meeting is crucial for our security," I admitted, persuasive. I didn't want to tell her the details of my business, but she might be more amenable if I reasoned with her. "And I promised my friends I would take care of things with Duarte and Rodríguez. I meant it when I said I don't break my promises, Evelyn. I made a promise to Gian and Enzo, but I'll make a vow to you too: I will do everything in my power to make you happy. I will take care of you and give you everything you desire."

"What I desire is to return home to Albuquerque." That defiant posture was back, her shoulders squared and her delicate chin tipped at an impertinent angle.

Surrendering to my darkest instincts, I cradled her nape and crushed my lips to hers, trapping her in a fierce kiss. She wouldn't be able to talk about leaving me if I tamed her tongue with mine. I would drive her wild with mindless passion, until she'd never consider being parted from me. I wanted to make her addicted to my touch, just as I was already addicted to her nearness.

I was usually skillful in my seductions, but the imbalance in my relationship with Evelyn made me feral. I was undeniably obsessed with her, and she was still thinking of returning to her life in America. Without me.

I would obliterate that desire from her mind and cleave her soul to mine. Just the thought of losing her robbed the air from my lungs, so I breathed her in instead, taking her oxygen as I kissed her in a ruthless claim. She softened in my arms, her tongue lashing mine in desperate strokes.

Her hips pressed tight to my thigh, and she shuddered against me in need. I'd left my good girl waiting long enough. I'd edged her before the party, teasing her pussy and tormenting us both to ensure her compliance. She'd done so well. I would show her how much she pleased me.

I should probably stay longer to entertain Duarte, but I couldn't hold back for another minute. The notorious hedonist would simply have to understand why I was leaving early. My fiery bond with Evelyn would be obvious enough to anyone watching our intense kiss. I staked my claim in front of everyone, brazen in my desire for this perfect woman.

All mine.

I finally released her swollen lips, and she swayed into me, dizzy from our heady chemistry. I braced my arm around her waist and steered her off the dance floor, away from the party.

"Time for your reward, *dolcezza*."

She shivered, and her cheeks flushed once again. She'd been indignant about my promise of a reward for good behavior, but Evelyn had a sweet heart and a giving nature. And I'd worked her into an erotic frenzy. It wouldn't be difficult to convince her to love being my good girl, to please me in every way I desired.

We stepped into the empty elevator that would carry us up to my suite. As soon as the doors closed, she threw herself at me like she was starved for my lips. Shock punched me, but I didn't hesitate to meet her hungry kiss with equal fervor. She pressed her hips against my thigh again, on the verge of rubbing herself against me to reach orgasm.

I slammed my palm against the emergency stop button, and the elevator came to a halt. She didn't seem to notice; she was completely intent on kissing me, her fingernails biting into the back of my neck in an effort to pull me closer.

"You are a greedy girl." My words were strangely slow and deep, like I was drunk. Everything about her was intoxicating, all-consuming.

I backed her up against the mirrored wall and wedged my thigh between her legs. "Go on," I ordered. "Make yourself feel good, *farfallina*."

She licked her lips, hesitating. She was so innocent. I found her shame delectable. I would find every wicked act that made her blush and teach her to love it.

I lifted my leg slightly, forcing her up onto her toes. I could feel the heat of her pussy through my pants, and I wondered if she'd come hard enough leave a wet spot on the expensive fabric.

The prospect made my cock stiffen. Fuck, I needed her. I craved to drive into that wet heat and feel her tight cunt squeezing me as she came undone.

I clenched my jaw and shoved down my most basic, animal urges. I wouldn't rut into her like a mindless beast. Evelyn would welcome me to claim her sweet pussy. She would beg me to fuck her. Until she was ready to do that, I would control my darkest instincts by dominating her. Controlling her pleasure helped me master myself too.

A heady rush of power pulsed through me as she began to rock against my thigh, stimulating herself at my command. Her eyes slid closed, as though she could hide from the shame that she was feeling for behaving so wantonly.

My fingers tangled in her hair, tugging just sharply enough to capture her full attention. Her stunning eyes met mine, glassy with lust. Using my grip on her hair, I directed her face toward the mirrored wall to our right.

"Watch yourself," I rumbled. "See how beautiful you are when you come undone for me."

"Massimo..." She whispered my name, a soft plea for mercy that made my cock ache.

But I had no mercy. She would bear witness to her own carnal desperation, her full submission to my will. I'd done this to her: reduced her to a needy, lustful mess. My power over her was the most delicious thing I'd ever seen.

When her eyes locked on her own reflection, her lips parted on a soft gasp, as though she didn't recognize herself. I pressed deeper into her, stimulating her clit on my thigh. She released a soft cry, then surrendered. Her hips rocked, her hot cunt rubbing against me. She blushed, but she stared at herself with rapt fascination as her breaths quickened and her movements became more frantic.

"Come, Evelyn. Come for me."

She shuddered in my arms and orgasmed with a low moan. I could practically feel the waves of bliss rolling through her body, almost as though her pleasure was my own.

"That's it," I praised, watching her reflection along with her. She remained transfixed by the image of her ecstatic abandon. "*Bellissima.*"

A soft whimper caught in her throat, and her body softened as she floated down from her orgasmic high.

But I wasn't nearly finished with her. Once I got her back to my bed, I would make her scream my name.

Chapter 20

Evelyn

The world took on a dreamlike quality in my post-orgasmic haze. Had that really been my reflection in the elevator mirror? I hadn't recognized the sensual woman who'd stared back at me while she rubbed against a near-stranger's thigh.

Objectively, I barely knew Massimo. The only fact I knew about him was that he worked with the Camorra. That alone should've repulsed me despite his physical appeal, but I couldn't help craving him.

Because I'd seen so much more to him. I was coming to understand the kind of man he was.

Massimo was a protector, a provider. He had a code of honor. And he cared about me deeply, perhaps so much that it should unnerve me.

But no one had ever looked at me like he did. No

one had ever treated me so well, like my happiness mattered to them. Not my family, and certainly not George.

My full, greedy focus remained centered on my dark protector as he quickly led me through the suite and into his bedroom. I followed without hesitation, not troubled by even a shred of fear at the prospect of being with him. He'd ignited a carnal fire inside me, and even though I'd just experienced the most powerful orgasm of my life, I craved more.

In that moment, I didn't think about escape; I didn't want to put any distance between us. I needed Massimo's hands on me, his scent enfolding me. I craved for his intoxicating kiss to consume all my worries so that I could simply revel in his nearness.

He picked me up and immediately tossed me down on the bed, so that I was sprawled in the center of the mattress. I tried to scramble into a more dignified position, but his hand splayed on the center of my chest, pinning me with steady pressure over my heart.

"Stay."

Even his orders didn't bother me now. I was too caught up in desire to feel any irritation. If obeying his command earned me more pleasure, I wouldn't try to resist or protest.

He dropped a quick, doting kiss on my forehead

before leaving me briefly to cross to the chest of drawers. Unease nipped at me when I saw the rope around his fist, but even that didn't stir true fear. He'd bound me before, and it hadn't caused me any pain.

"What's that for?" I asked. "I'm not trying to run away, Massimo."

He shot me a crooked grin that made my heart skip a beat. "I know you're not, *farfallina*. You're being very good for me. But I want to bind you. I want you at my mercy, so I can play with you however I desire. Don't worry. I'll make sure you love every second in my ropes."

"Oh," I breathed, shocked by his dirty promises. The filthy things he said to me were perverse, deviant.

And I'd never been more turned on.

I wasn't entirely naïve; I knew plenty of people enjoyed kinky sex. I'd just never thought I was one of them. I'd never thought much of sex at all, really. It was just something people did for their partner in a relationship, a way to keep men happy. I'd never really understood what all the fuss was about.

Until now. Until Massimo.

The rope wound around my wrists in a slightly rough caress. I didn't resist as he bound me to the bedposts, my arms stretched above my head. I simply watched him with rapt fascination: the smooth, practiced way he handled the rope and the shape of his huge, masculine hands that tied it so deftly.

When my arms were secured, he took a moment to stare down at me, as though I was an equally fascinating creature, something strange and ethereal. Painfully perfect to look upon.

He traced the lines of my cheekbones, the curve of my jaw, the shape of my lower lip—memorizing me. His fingertips imprinted his heat on me with each tender brush, the touch possessive and reverent.

The tender moment turned suddenly savage when he fisted my dress in those big hands. The silk tore, exposing me the same way he'd stripped his shirt off me at the breakfast table. This dress probably cost a lot more than that t-shirt, but he didn't seem to care about destroying the expensive garment. He stared at me as though seeing my naked body was the most valuable thing in his world. His flame blue eyes seared into my soul, peering straight into the core of who I was. Whatever he saw in me, it made his beautiful lips curve in masculine satisfaction.

"Are you still aching for me, Evelyn?" he asked, voice rough with his own suppressed lust.

"Yes." I nearly moaned at the sound of my name in his deep, accented voice. That sound alone would've made me wet, but my thighs were already slick from arousal. It would've embarrassed me, but Massimo's nostrils flared like a predator who'd just scented his prey.

"Fuck, I can't wait to taste you again."

He positioned himself between my thighs, his broad shoulders spreading me wide. His face was so close to my heated sex; I could feel each of his warm breaths on my desire-slicked skin. My clit pulsed madly, but he didn't touch me where I needed it most. He studied my most intimate area as though it was a priceless work of art, a treasure to be coveted.

"What a pretty pussy," he purred, the praise vibrating over my swollen folds. "And it's all mine."

I squeezed my eyes shut, as though I could hide from the intensity of his lustful gaze. I jerked against the ropes, instinctively trying to cover myself. Instead of inciting panic, the sense of complete helplessness to resist him only stoked my lust. There was no room for modesty with Massimo. He wouldn't allow anything to separate us, not even social decorum. His deviance freed me in a way I'd never known, and I became a being of pure carnal desire.

"Look at me while I make you come," he ordered.

My eyes snapped open, immediately finding his molten gaze. He kept me locked in his flame blue stare as he licked my sex in a long, lewd lave of his tongue.

He groaned as though I was the most delicious thing he'd ever tasted, and he began feasting on me like he was starving for me. Like he was a man possessed by the singular need to learn every caress and flick that made me moan.

"Massimo. Massimo, Massimo..." I began panting his name in a litany, like a prayer. This beautiful man was more than my protector: he was my new god.

"That's it," he urged, stroking me to a frenzy. "Scream my name, *dolcezza*."

He sucked on my clit, and I had no choice but to obey. His name was ripped from somewhere deep in my chest, a primal, visceral release. Ecstasy exploded through my body, igniting at my core and rushing out in a shockwave to my fingers and toes. I writhed, completely lost in bliss. His fingers dug into my thighs, pinning me in place as he continued to feast on me.

My clit was so sensitive, the pleasure morphing into a keen pain that was almost unbearable. I whined and tried to wriggle away from his mouth.

Fresh pain bloomed on my inner thigh. Massimo had captured me in another wicked bite. This time, it was a punishment for trying to evade him.

I cried out, but the pain was over. He kissed the mark and returned his attention to my pussy.

"I'm not finished," he growled, then settled back between my legs.

I wasn't sure how long the sweet torment continued, and I lost track of my orgasms. When my throat was hoarse from screaming his name, and all I could do was whimper and give him every last drop of my pleasure, he finally relented.

He loomed over me, the world a bliss-filled haze around him. All I could focus on were his stunning eyes and the masculine perfection of his beautiful face. I heard the sound of his belt unbuckling, and my gaze lowered to his impressive erection. He fisted his thick cock, hissing his own pleasure as he touched himself.

I jerked weakly against my restraints, wanting to touch him the way he'd touched me.

His palm pressed down on my belly, just above my sex. "Stay still, *farfallina*. I'm going to mark you."

His hot cum lashed my breasts, and a different kind of pleasure glowed in the center of my chest. My satisfaction was more than just physical; I'd made this powerful beast of a man come undone. He'd taken control of my body, my pleasure. He'd staked his claim over me, and now, he was marking me as his.

"*Mine*," he snarled, lips peeled back from his white teeth in a purely primal expression.

The corners of my eyes stung. No one had ever

looked at me like that. No one had ever wanted me so desperately. Like I was everything to him, and he would do anything to possess me. It should alarm me, but I was too drunk on bliss to be scared. I'd been alone for so long, and Massimo wasn't letting me hide from him. He kept me exactly where he wanted me: in his arms, under his protection.

His mouth crashed down on mine, and he branded my lips with a soul-searing kiss.

Chapter 21

Evelyn

"I still don't want to go to Colombia," I told Massimo honestly on our way to the airport the next morning, as though I could somehow convince him to turn the SUV around and take me...

Where? Where did I want to go?

Not back to Stefano Duarte's home, the heart of a dangerous cartel.

Not back to the shabby, cramped apartment I'd shared with George in Mexico City.

Back to Albuquerque? Where I didn't have any friends, my family didn't care about me, and the future I'd envisioned with George was in ruins?

The realization had tormented me all morning, ever since I'd woken up in Massimo's arms.

"Don't ask me to let you go," he said, a low warning. He slung his arm over me, pulling me closer. "You're staying with me. I thought we agreed last night. You're mine."

Mine.

My heart squeezed as I remembered the way he'd made me feel last night, when he'd tied me to his bed and marked me as his. No one had ever wanted me so desperately, not even George. With him, I'd constantly sought his affection and approval. Massimo lavished me with affection, even when I protested. And he was so generous with his praise that I didn't know how to handle all of the positive affirmations and compliments.

"I don't want..." I stopped myself before I could say that I didn't want him to let me go. That was insane. A mafioso was about to take me to meet with a cartel boss in Colombia, and I didn't want to leave him.

It might be insane, but I couldn't deny my conflicted feelings for him.

"I know you'll keep me safe," I said instead. "But I don't want to go to Colombia. I don't want anything to do with the cartels."

He shrugged. "It's just business, *dolcezza*. You don't need to worry about any of that. I'll make sure you enjoy yourself."

Before I could formulate another protest, he cupped my breast in a brazen caress.

"Massimo!" I tried to squirm away, mortified. We were in the backseat of the SUV, and the driver would be able to see him touching me if he glanced in the rearview mirror.

"You don't need to worry about anything, Evelyn. I'll take care—"

"Massimo!" I screamed his name in the moment before the van smashed into the side of our SUV.

Tires screeched, glass shattered, and pain exploded through my skull.

The world wavered around me, and my head ached. I shook it to clear away the ringing in my ears, but it didn't quite work. I blinked, willing everything to stop spinning.

I cried his name again when I saw the blood covering Massimo's beautiful face. His stunning eyes were closed, his powerful body slumped in the seat. The impact had been on his side of the SUV, and he'd taken the worst of the collision.

Before I could reach for him, the car door was wrenched open beside me, and rough hands grabbed me. Strange men dragged me out of the ruined SUV, away from Massimo, who was terribly still. Was he breathing?

He couldn't be dead. He couldn't be.

I screamed for him and twisted against the iron hold of the men who were taking me away from the wreck.

"Calm down, you dumb bitch," one of them barked.

"Let me go," I insisted, struggling to get back to Massimo. We neared another unmarked white van—not an emergency response vehicle. "Who are you?" I demanded, a fresh burst of fear punching my chest.

"We're friends of your fiancé. He asked us to get you back for him. He didn't say in what condition."

My blood ran cold, and I began fighting like a wildcat, mindless with terror. George had sent these men. They would take me back to him, and he would kill me. He'd almost let me be gunned down right in front of him, all to keep his corruption secret.

But I wasn't strong enough to resist my captors, not powerful like my dark protector.

Massimo.

All that blood on his beautiful face...

I screamed and kicked, fighting to get back to him.

One of my assailants cursed, and my world went white with a burst of pain across my cheek. My vision darkened, and my body sagged. My last thought as the door of the van closed behind me was of Massimo, wondering if my savior was alive.

Fear for him followed me down into oblivion.

Thank you for reading TAINTED OBSESSION! I hope you loved this first installment in the King of Ruin Trilogy. Massimo and Evelyn's story continues in ILLICIT OBSESSION.

Want more dark and kinky mafia romance? Stefano Duarte and Carmen Ronaldo's steamy, suspenseful story is available now in WICKED KING!

Wicked King Excerpt

Carmen

I might have signed my own death warrant, but it was too late to stop what I'd put in motion. My heart hammered against the inside of my ribcage, pumping adrenaline through my body. The resultant rush sent a strange sense of giddiness soaring through my system. Despite the terror twisting my stomach into knots, I swallowed a bizarre laugh.

I pressed my sweaty palm against the cool metal of the reinforced steel door, the crack in the defensive wall that protected my family estate. The thick barrier was meant to shield me from the enemy outside, but I was about to unlock the door and welcome them into the fortress that had kept me safe for over a decade.

I took a deep breath, straightened my spine, and wrapped my fingers around the door handle. Bracing myself to face the enemy, I hauled the heavy metal barrier inward, creating a breach in the walls that had been erected to withstand a siege.

But it wasn't only my enemy waiting on the other side.

My nightmare stared back at me, his black eyes glinting with malicious pleasure and his sensual lips split in a cruel grin.

My heart leapt into my throat, and I threw my weight against the heavy door, desperate to lock out the man who haunted my dreams: Stefano Duarte, vicious drug lord and my own personal demon.

I barely noticed the blood-soaked, hulking brute who accompanied him; I didn't register my enemy, Mateo Ignazio, as a threat. We had a truce in place.

I had no such bargain arranged to protect me from Stefano.

But as I'd feared, it was too late to change my mind. The steel door didn't give quickly enough under my weight, and my attempt to close it only incited my enemy to violent action.

Ignazio barreled toward me, his huge body slamming the metal inward. The impact shoved the air from my lungs and propelled me backward, knocking me off-balance. Cool, damp grass cushioned my fall, and the stars of the night sky filled my vision. The sudden shift in my perspective disoriented me, my mind reeling from the physical fall and the visceral fear incited by Stefano's presence.

I gasped in air, preparing to scream for help. This had been a terrible mistake.

Ignazio had promised he would only bring a small team of men with him to aid in this operation: rescuing the woman he loved, Sofia, from my cruel brother, Pedro. Ignazio would get Sofia back, and I would arrange a targeted coup, taking control of my family's cartel for myself.

But that was before I'd known one of the men would be Stefano Duarte. Panic clawed at my brain, obliterating rational thought.

I barely finished filling my lungs with oxygen when a heavy weight settled over my body, pressing me deeper into the earth. Strong hands ensnared my wrists, forcing them together above my head and pinning me to the ground. A warm, calloused palm clamped over my parted lips, smothering my scream.

For a moment, he was a silhouette against the night sky, his darkness blotting out the stars. My vision adjusted in the dim lighting, and I could make out his sculpted, angular features, rendered sharper and more terrifying by the shadows pooling beneath his high cheekbones. His black eyes captured a glimmer of moonlight, making them glitter with malicious pleasure. White teeth flashed in a predatory smile.

My body recognized the scent I thought I'd forgotten: rich, earthy tobacco sharpened by exotic spice. It filled my senses, and a flash of remembered heat radiated through my body. The involuntary reaction fueled my fear.

No part of me should desire Stefano Duarte. He used his beauty to lure in his prey, and I'd vowed never to fall into his trap again.

Unfortunately, it seemed a deep, shameful corner of my psyche craved the ecstasy of his masterful touch.

No! I wasn't the naïve young woman who'd fallen into his arms all those years ago. I knew better now than to trust any man. Stefano had been the first to teach me that painful lesson.

Blind panic and rage caused my muscles to tense and jerk against his powerful hold. I'd spent more than a decade learning to defend myself, but one glance at Stefano had been so jarring that all my training left my brain. It was too late for that now; he had me pinned, his muscular body trapping me beneath him.

His cruelly gorgeous face dipped toward mine, as though he intended to claim a kiss. But his hand was still firmly pressed over my lips, silencing my scream. He leaned in to whisper in my ear, his masculine scent invading my senses.

"Quiet now, kitten," he purred, his warm breath fanning my neck.

I stilled, tense and trembling. Terror rode me hard, but warmth pooled low in my belly.

"You promised to help my friend Mateo. Remember?" he prompted. His low rumble was seductive as ever, capturing my focus and guiding me back to rational thought.

A feral growl pulled my attention fully to the present. My gaze slid past Stefano to find Mateo Ignazio glaring down at me. His eyes were dark with wild fury, his lips peeled back from his teeth in an animal snarl. He had come to my family's estate to rescue Sofia, and his fear for her had driven him to the brink of madness. Ignazio was little more than a beast on his best days. I'd heard what he was capable of. I shuddered to think what he might do to me if I tried to keep him from Sofia now that I'd allowed him to break past my home's defenses.

It appeared the only thing holding him back from attacking me was the restraining arm of Adrián Rodríguez, the notoriously sadistic Colombian drug lord who ruled over all of us. Without his product to traffic through Mexico and into the United States, cartels like mine and Stefano's wouldn't possess a quarter of the wealth we currently had at our disposal.

Rodríguez's personal presence in this extraction mission cooled the heat that Stefano had incited in my blood. I knew Rodríguez had a close personal relationship with Ignazio, who served as his bodyguard. But if the Devil himself had chosen to enter my home, along with Stefano Duarte, this situation was far more deadly and capricious than I'd realized.

"Tell Mateo where he can find Sofia, and this will all be over soon." Stefano's voice was at my ear, his murmured words sinking inside me and offering perverse comfort. "I will leave your home, and you won't be harmed tonight."

His soothing tone grounded me, even though his nearness should horrify me. The sudden turn of events in an already tense scenario was fucking with my cognitive abilities.

"I gave you my word," Rodríguez reminded me, his pale green, panther's eyes gleaming through the darkness.

I swallowed hard, my mind struggling to function beyond a primal, fear-based level.

You have my word. Rodríguez's promise echoed

through my mind. *You control the Ronaldo Cartel now, Carmen. Tell us how we can access your estate.*

We'd struck that bargain less than half an hour ago, when I'd called him and arranged this deal: access to my estate for Ignazio to rescue Sofia and kill my brother, and in exchange, I would be supported as the new head of the Ronaldo family cartel.

If anyone in my organization suspected that I had a hand in helping Ignazio kill my brother, I'd get a bullet in my brain. The only way I could maintain the power that Rodríguez offered was if Pedro's associates and small army of loyal men believed that I was the most effective leader for our organization. Rodríguez's support would ensure my position, but only if my subterfuge remained secret.

I wouldn't be the one to wield the knife, but ultimately, Pedro's demise would be at my hands. The bastard would be dead within the hour, and I would have more than I'd ever dared to dream: power, respect, security.

I just had to gather my wits and navigate the altered scenario. Stefano and Rodríguez might be inside my protective fortress alongside Ignazio, but that didn't mean the terms of our deal had changed. All I had to do was guide the men to my brother, and then I could claim the control that would ensure my survival.

Keeping my eyes locked on Rodríguez, I managed a small nod, moving my head as much as I was able with Stefano's hand pressed against my mouth.

The bastard's low hum of approval rumbled against my chest, sinking deeper into my body to spark the heat my terror had doused.

He dropped a doting, mocking kiss on the tip of my nose, as though expressing pride in me for good behavior.

Rage swelled, the furious burn eclipsing the disconcerting, sensual heat he'd stirred inside me. This was how Stefano operated: he toyed with his prey. He found it amusing to manipulate me, twisting me in knots before disengaging with an arrogant smile.

His weight lifted from my body, leaving me free to move and speak. Once he got to his feet, he held out a hand, offering to help me up with his signature gentlemanly veneer.

Only a fool would fall for his false smiles and gentility. I wasn't a fool. Not anymore.

I scowled at him and stood up without his assistance, only wobbling slightly as I found my balance. All my instincts for self-preservation screamed at me to keep my eyes on Stefano, but I needed to display strength to the predators around me. I was one of them, and I had to remind them of my own personal power.

They might all be physically stronger than me, but I was outranked only by Rodríguez in this little group. Ignazio was technically beneath me, even if he could snap my neck with one hand. And once my brother was dead and the Ronaldo Cartel was mine, Stefano Duarte would be my equal.

At least, he would be until I eliminated him. As soon as I had my own organization firmly under my control, I would make it my life's mission to rid myself of Stefano once and for all. The rival drug lord wouldn't live out the year, not if I had anything to say about it.

I lifted my chin and turned away from the men, doing my best to suppress the sickening unease incited by having all of them at my back.

"This way," I urged, relieved when my voice came out in my usual cool, clipped tones.

They followed where I led, all of us moving soundlessly over the lushly manicured lawn. Dozens of armed men guarded the perimeter around the estate, but with this small team safely inside the walls, I knew exactly which path to take and which shadows to move through in order to reach the mansion without alarming security.

Pedro had extra muscle posted tonight, prepared for a full-scale siege. He'd known that kidnapping Sofia would bring Ignazio's—and therefore Rodríguez's—wrath down upon our organization. But my brother was arrogant, his entitlement blinding him to the severe risks he'd taken. He thought he could topple Rodríguez himself, but this power grab would be the last conceited mistake he'd ever make. Daddy wasn't around to save his golden heir now.

All that extra manpower that Pedro had paid so dearly to protect his pathetic life wouldn't be of any use to him now. Most of the guards were posted at the fringes of the estate, and there would be far fewer men inside the mansion to shield my brother from Ignazio's feral wrath.

I could practically feel his tense menace pulsing over me, his impatience to save the woman he loved.

My stomach turned at the thought of Sofia with my brother, and I picked up the pace. I couldn't risk a show of womanly weakness, but my fear for what he might do to the unwilling girl had forced my hand in enacting this coup. I never would have dared this bold course of action solely for my own power. Even with the backing of Adrián Rodríguez, this clandestine takeover of the Ronaldo Cartel wasn't without risk. One misstep would earn me a knife in the back.

But I'd seen the way my brother had handled Sofia. He wasn't going to give her a choice. Even now, I might be too late. He might have forced himself on her already.

My stomach lurched, and cold sweat beaded on the back of my neck.

I drew in a long breath through my nose and blew it out through my mouth, practicing the breathing exercises that helped me cling to sanity when dark memories threatened to take over my brain.

By the time we reached the mansion, the familiar panic symptoms ebbed, granting me more control over my thoughts and physiological responses.

I'd chosen to access the house via a back entrance into a mudroom usually used by our groundskeepers. This wing of the sprawling manor was mostly dark, none of the rooms currently in use. Pedro had evicted all guests and even close associates prior to kidnapping Sofia. He hadn't trusted that they wouldn't turn on him during this tumultuous time.

None of my brother's men would have dared to raise a hand against him. Until I saw how he intended to treat Sofia, I wouldn't have dared to challenge him, either.

Now, he would pay for his years of casual cruelty.

And I would finally be safe.

I paused at the bottom of a stairwell that was used only by household management staff. No one would be here at this time of night, and the minimal security posted around my brother's bedroom could be easily handled by the vicious killers at my back.

I turned to face them, keeping my eyes fixed on Rodríguez. Addressing him was a strategic show of respect to the most powerful man in the group. But focusing solely on him also allowed me to mitigate the debilitating fear elicited by Stefano's nearness.

"Security is lax this deep into the compound, so you should be able to navigate from here without me," I informed him in an undertone.

If I was going to feign innocence in my brother's murder, I couldn't risk being seen anywhere near him.

Rodríguez listened intently to my descriptions of the guards' locations and the resistance they might face. His eerie, luminous eyes glowed through the darkness, his keen attention making the fine hairs on the back of my neck rise.

I resisted the urge to drop my gaze and back away.

He gave me his word, I reminded myself. Rodríguez might be a sadistic monster, but he kept his promises. By morning, Pedro would be dead, and I would control the Ronaldo Cartel.

"Pedro's bedroom is on the third floor." I killed my brother with a few words. "There will be two guards in the hall. Others will come running if they hear a disturbance."

"Then it's a good thing they'll be distracted by an external assault," Rodríguez drawled. His mouth quirked in a cruel smirk, and he offered me a sardonic nod. "Enjoy being Queen of the Ashes."

"What?" The disbelieving gasp barely left my lips before Stefano grabbed me from behind.

His calloused palm clamped over my mouth, silencing me once again. His other arm was an iron band around my middle, pinning my elbows at either side of my waist. He pulled me tightly against him, so I could feel every hard line of his body.

"I promised I would leave your home if you were good, kitten," he murmured, his words hot against the cold sweat on my skin. "And I'll keep my promise. I'm leaving, and you're coming with me."

I screamed into his hand, twisting in his grip. The bastard laughed, his low chuckle rich with amusement.

"Being Queen of the Ashes doesn't sound like much fun," he mused, nuzzling my hair and inhaling the scent of my fear. "You'll be much happier as my pet." He nipped at my ear, stoking my terror with a little edge of pain. "Once I've tamed you."

Also by Julia Sykes

The Captive Series

Sweet Captivity

Claiming My Sweet Captive

Stealing Beauty

Captive Ever After

Pretty Hostage

Wicked King

Ruthless Savior

Eternally His

King of Ruin

Tainted Obsession

Illicit Obsession

Endless Obsession

The Impossible Series

Impossible

Savior

Rogue

Knight

Mentor

Master

King

A Decadent Christmas (An Impossible Series Christmas Special)

Czar

Crusader

Prey (An Impossible Series Short Story)

Highlander

Decadent Knights (An Impossible Series Short Story)

Centurion

Dex

Hero

Wedding Knight (An Impossible Series Short Story)

Valentines at Dusk (An Impossible Series Short Story)

Nice & Naughty (An Impossible Series Christmas Special)

Dark Lessons

Mafia Ménage Trilogy

Mafia Captive

The Daddy and The Dom

Theirs to Protect

Their Captive Bride

In Their Hands

In Their Power

In Their Hearts

Fallen Mafia Prince Trilogy

Fallen Prince

Stolen Princess

Fractured Kingdom